42 DAYS OF LOVE

About the author

Vikas Trivedi hails from Dungarpur, a small town near Udaipur in Rajasthan. Having struggled with studies as a child, he took it as a challenge to conquer his weakness and went on to achieve a Master's Degree in individual streams of English Literature, Psychology and Political Science, and a PhD in Psychology. He now uses his knowledge and education to teach, as a professor of Psychology and Literature. Apart from teaching, he also enjoys playing sports, reading, meditation, yoga and exercise.

His debut book, *The Hidden Spark*, intends to enlighten and teach its readers about the powers of the mind, the strength of self-motivation, ways to unleash one's potential, and more.

He found inspiration for his new book when he met an ocean diver from California. Vikas was touched and inspired by her heroic life, and was determined to immortalize her story through his words.

Vikas Trivedi

About the co-author

Smita Agarwal, the co-author, hails from Kolkata, West Bengal. Even as a child, her interests steered into creative art. She pursued Honours in Accountancy and after having graduated, she gave in to her passion for creative work. She ventured into the field of Interior Designing and received a diploma in Computer Aided Designing.

Smita also happens to be an extremely knowledgeable and successful Pranic healer, an art she has been practicing for over 13 years. The continual study of Pranic healing is what led her into exploring the powers of the mind, and finally meeting Vikas Trivedi. The two of them together went on to write their debut book, *The Hidden Spark*.

Smita Agarwal

Praise for the authors and their work

"...an embodiment of various emotions, research, fallacies and inspiration transforming every bit of our life."

– *Aaj Tak*

"This book will make you believe that there is life after death, success after failures and hope after the darkest night..."

– *Kevin Missal, author of best-selling book* Kalki

"Motivating story... a chance to achieve what they dream of..."

– *Navjyoti Times*

"A remarkable and impeccably formulated book."

– *News Now*

"...enter deep into readers' hearts, heal them and inspire them..."

– *Rashtradoot*

"...your go-to resource when you feel lost figuring out life"

– *Rajasthan Patrika*

"...a transforming tale of courage, hope and self-discovery."

– *Prabhat Kiran*

"A wonderful book that motivates you in a very practical way..."

– *Udaipur Kiran*

"...overwhelming and enthralling piece of fiction."

– *Radio City, Jaipur*

42 DAYS OF LOVE

VIKAS TRIVEDI
SMITA AGARWAL

Srishti
PUBLISHERS & DISTRIBUTORS

Srishti Publishers & Distributors
Registered Office: N-16, C.R. Park
New Delhi – 110 019
Corporate Office: 212A, Peacock Lane
Shahpur Jat, New Delhi – 110 049
editorial@srishtipublishers.com

First published by
Srishti Publishers & Distributors in 2019

10 9 8 7 6 5 4 3 2 1

Printed and bound in India

Introduction

"Greatest treasures are always guarded by the cruelest of dragons..."

Legends have it that the ocean buries some of the greatest secrets and treasures in its heart. In the deep, dark depths of the Indian Ocean, located far into the Bay of Bengal, North Sentinel Island is one of the most isolated places on earth. It has remained almost entirely cut off from the world. The Sentinel islands hold a treasure too great for any one man. Some call this place the Blue Hole, others simply mention it as the waters of death. Surrounded by a group of small islands, it ranges over 59.67 km^2 (14,700) in area. The Blue Hole is said to be 4200 fathoms deep (7681 metres). The horror, however, is not the depth. In the 1600s, a merchant ship from Portugal, Nossa Senhora Sebastiao, left from southern India. The crew had loaded the ship with gold, gems, and spices from the Nizam's (the greatest ruler of princely states of India) convoy along the shoreline. As Nizam was terrified of a revolution taking place, he made plans to transport his wealth out of the country, all ready to be traded in Portugal. But something went wrong on the way and the ship never reached Portugal.

Years later, debris of an old ship close to an island of the Sentinel group was reported by a navy chopper. It was said that the crew hit a terrible sea-storm. An investigation by the mariners revealed that the ship had never sunk. Portuguese crew members, in an attempt to lighten the vessel, unloaded all its treasure into the ocean. Anticipating the horrors of the ship sinking, they escaped via wooden lifeboats. The crew was never found again. But years later, 'Sebastiao' uncovered itself before the world. Several marine expeditions were launched in order to find the missing treasure. Nautical historians claim that the ship carried over forty tons of gold at the time. Judging by the route Sebastiao was supposed to take, and where it was discovered, it was deduced that the unloaded treasure should lie somewhere in a trench near the Blue Hole.

Multiple expedition teams tried their luck; even the best of treasure hunters were called. The attempts only stopped after a few deep divers failed to surface, as they faced spine-chilling storms A lesser-known reason for the horror was discovered later when ships anchored near the main Sentinel island. The place was and still is populated by a primitive tribe, sixty thousand years old, isolated from the world, known as the Sentinelese. The tribe is hostile and has butchered many sailors who stepped on to the island unknowingly.

Sebastiao's treasure lies within a narrowed down area of 17 nautical square miles. The barrier here is not depth, as the divers who managed to surface and beat the immense hydrostatic pressure tell, "The place is an underwater network of caves, crevices, and strange life-forms, darkness, unbearable pressure, anxiety, no oxygen, and one shot are enough to restore anyone's faith in god again."

I am Donna, a professional diver, explorer and a problem solver. I hail from an ordinary family of fishermen. The sea has always fascinated me like my family, but in a different way. My parents earned a living through the sea; I earn my life from it. I took up diving to unwind myself and find my soul again. At the age of sixteen, I went aboard a battleship with two of my friends. The metal, the grit, the freedom and the thrills of ocean diving drove me to be a deep sea diver.

I have always been the ambitious kind, the one who wants fame and wealth. I might sound selfish, though I have never been dishonest with anyone. I come from a dysfunctional family where happiness was rare.

'Where is the torch?' I thought to myself. As I woke up from the blackout, I recollected faint trails of the thoughts running in my mind. I removed the snorkel and the mask. A little tearing over the head cover of the suit indicated a cut. I was bleeding. Not profusely, but it was scary enough. I couldn't hear a thing; my ears were clogged. Thank god! I was in an air-pocket inside a cave, but not for long.

I could only see with my mask-light. Upon frantically searching for a torch, I found one. Just one switch and the air-pocket got lit up with lumens of bright light. Sometimes you do not like what you see around you. My oxygen tank indicated a few minutes of the gas. My knee was also hurt. I remembered radioing in the crew about the dive.

My navigation system was broken too. No direction, only a few minutes of oxygen, and a hurt body, I thought to myself. 'Seems like my life in brief.' It seemed to me like time was replaying itself by placing horrible conditions ahead of me and asking, What now little girl? Many tough situations have crossed my path; each stronger than the last one. But I was resilient; at least I like to believe so. But now I was broken. Time is the biggest bully of all. Too many failed attempts break your soul.

I was unable to contact the crew. This little cave was cozy. No sound, little light, and the sound of water seeping in from the roof, holding millions of tons of water above it.

The search for the ship Sebastiao's treasure bought me here. As I overheard the conversation between Dr John Clenton, a former head of Arafura and Timor Seas Ecosystem Australia (ATSEA) and the senior chief of Sydney Harbour Federation and Fisheries Department. I got all the layer details from their conversation. Sometimes a series of clues lead you to a new purpose or a new situation. It wasn't only the force of ambition that drove me. The reasons for my action went down too deep, entangled in my past, and meeting somewhere in my future. I was stuck in the middle. And, there waited my crew in N45 Tambor Class expedition submarine, probably not aware of my life-and-death situation.

This treasure was supposed to be my freedom from the past, sense of fulfillment inside me, and an aid to a special humanitarian mission that had always been my dream. 'Time cannot be that big a jerk,' I thought to myself.

"Let's go!" I shouted to boost up my confidence. I grabbed the gear, and decided to stand. I just needed a plan out of here to stay alive.

I used to think of myself as Andrew Potter's, my father's, treasure. Up until the age of eight years, I saw a hero in my dad. To me, he was a huge masculine figure whom I copied at every step. He was someone who I could look up to. My world was a small bubble, and he just lay outside of it. My mother Catherine Potter was a sweet-spoken, god-fearing lady of high religious values, who never left me out of her sight. She wouldn't let me spend too much time with my dad. I thought she was taking away the affection and attention I deserved. I used to think she was jealous of all the attention I got from dad.

I remember, one day, when I was eight or so, I saw a beast of immense strength, hyper-aggressive and destructive. It was my father. I came down to the living room on hearing some noises. Mom and dad were arguing. I had heard them screaming, yelling and cursing each other. I sneaked down from the stairs, trying to check out what was going on. My heart pounded as I drew near to my fighting parents. Then I heard a loud thud, something dark and heavy. That darkness, that feeling never really left me. I heard mom groan, and sob. I saw my father holding mom by her hair. I saw her face, she had tears, she was in pain, but she had anger in her eyes. I could sense her anger; suddenly my father hit her hard across her face. She fell on the floor.

This incident changed most of the things for me, forever. Those fights grew worse as the years passed. We became aliens living under the same roof. Father never stopped drinking; mom never stopped resisting him and loving me. I was nineteen when I realized a great thing. It was about my mom. The silent burning anger I saw in her eyes that night was not anger at all; it was courage. It was survival, love and hope at the same time. I knew for sure that I had my mother's survival instinct in me and I was meant tc survive.

My ambitions became higher and stronger. The goals became clearer. *Donna Potter, you are made for something worth the pain.* That thought kept me going. I found myself to be a junior swimming trainer at the age of twenty-four. That was a confusing time though! Some of my friends were getting married, some pursuing higher education, some even having children, and others cherishing the youthful golden days of their life. On the contrary, I dreamt of the deep blue ocean and diving, only me, my equipment, and my mom's survival instinct. Rest of the world meant very little to me.

A note from the authors

Life is a story. Life is an adventure. The only difference is how you look upon it. It might not be a happy ending always. It might not be a failure all the time. Life is unpredictable. That becomes all the more reason to chase our dreams and achieve our goals. Our dreams and goals are tied to our very sense of existence. They broadly represent our true nature, our outlook of the world. At least this is what Donna believes.

A diver by profession, explorer by choice, Donna sets her sail to hunt for one of the most precious treasures of the human history. Gathering a crew of four experts on an old yet powerful submarine, she finds herself close to the North Sentinel island, the supposed home of the treasure. The team's incessant expedition towards the great treasure unites them to face massive dangers.

It, however, becomes clear to Donna that it is not just a battle of will. She finds herself trapped amidst deception, cheating, life threats, and ruthless situations bad enough to corrupt an innocent mind. Along the journey, she discovers her love, finds and loses trustworthy souls. But it seems like nobody can break her tough soul. Having been through emotional and physical traumas in the past, hailing from a dysfunctional family, and torn between passion and expectations, Donna seems to have seen it all.

And it is this learning that keeps Donna in the drive mode. Her story, however, is not at all a 'go get it with positivity and motivation' cliché. What happens to her and her love, in the end, will change your perspective on life

Does she find the treasure? Only she can tell. But before starting this thought-provoking journey of a lifetime, there is one advice for you.

Expect the unexpected during these 42 earth-shaking events.

42 Days of Love

On 4th August 1784, the ship named "The Royal Fortune" left from southern India with gold, gems, and spices, from the Nizam's convoy along the shoreline. As the Nizam was terrified of a revolution, he made plans to transport his wealth out of the country. But something went wrong on the way. The ship never reached Portugal. The pirates looted the ship and in an attempt to lighten the vessel and not sink with the load, unloaded all its excess treasure into the ocean.

Nautical historians claim that the ship carried over 2,600,000 gold pagoda coins, 173 magnificent pieces of jewels studded with pearls, diamonds, rubies and sapphires and other precious stones embedded in gold, and 17 tons of silver bars.

Multiple expedition teams tried their luck, even the best of treasure hunters from Woods Hole Oceangraphic Institution (WHOI) and a team from UNESCO were called. The attempts only stopped after a few deep divers failed to surface, as they faced spine-chilling storms, and all who went to get it never came back alive.

For now, the treasure itself remains where it has been for the last 250 years – resting on the sea bed.

Day 1

"Delay is always better than distress."

Sundays are bright. A vibrant shopping complex, food carts, birds chirping, children playing and the sun shining. Marfi Square is one of my favourite places to recharge myself. 'There she is,' I thought. Sonia greeted me with a warm smile, for which she was well known. Her dreamy eyes looked at me through her frameless spectacles, while she made her lean body rest on the cafe's chair. "Hey, Donna! Long time," she said, excitingly. One could easily spot how glad she was, and how gorgeous she looked in the orange top and black jeans.

"It is always a cheer to meet you, darling." I complimented her.

We waited for the three other members. "Others are joining us today, right?" asked Sonia.

"Yup! Anytime," I replied.

The cafe smelled like freshly ground mocha, and so we ordered two. "There they are!" said Sonia while gazing at someone approaching from my back. It was Anish and Samira.

They greeted us with a smile, shook our hands and made themselves comfortable. Our heads started reading each other as soon as we met. “Shall we start?” asked Anish.

“We have one more member coming in,” I replied while checking out my phone.

“Oh! I see,” exclaimed Anish.

“There is the devil,” said Sonia. I immediately knew he was there. Deceiving, handsome, intelligent, quick, no dressing sense at all. Well, it was David. That crooked smile made it hard to guess his intentions. It was his secret weapon.

“Hey guys! How is life?” I pulled out a map of the Indian Ocean, and unrolled it on the table, while Sonia and Anish shifted the coffee cups. “We all are here because forty tons of gold is haunting us in our dreams,” joked David in his signature evil style.

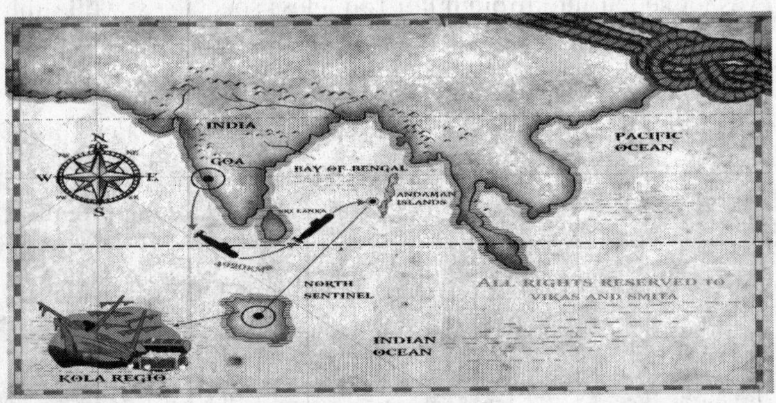

“Alright, guys! We have less than twenty days approximately to reach our target destination through the submarine. The location is Kola Regio, located a few miles north of the main

North Sentinal islands." I briefed the team members through the final session.

All the arrangements were in place. Right now, we were in Goa, approximately 4920 km from the target. The team obviously needed some crucial details to prepare themselves mentally. "The hidden treasure where the ship sank is 43.2km away from Sentinel island, in a place known as Kola Regio. It's identifiable by its contrasting deep dark blue colour alongside lighter shallower colours. With its incredibly strong currents is the sheer number of sharks found here. As it can get extremely dark in places, it causes divers disorientation and they tend to get lost, which is the main reason for many deaths at this site. Sonia, please run us through the equipment checklist," I requested her.

She then spoke out the checklist while I went through some more details that the team needed. "Oxygen tanks, auxiliary tanks, check! Snorkel, scuba mask, wetsuit, check! Diving watch and computer, check! GPS, check! Radio, check! SOS-Flares check!" Sonia spared no equipment.

Anish, David, Samira and I had all the crucial equipments and devices. I then asked David to brief the team about the submarine details.

David stood up and looked at his watch. "Well! Here is the plan. We have a privately rented submarine, an N45 Tambor class vessel from the Military Service Group. They have stationed the vessel near the port of Eden. Once we are there, a raft will lead us to the sub with all our equipment." David delivered his instructions in a professional manner. "Guys! Let's pack up and leave. We will meet at the port in four hours," said David.

"It's going to be one hell of a ride!" Anish cheered all of us. We were ready to undertake the mission of our lifetimes.

I was sobbing, feeling heavy, and even angry at some point. Goodbyes are always the hardest. The faces that you loved so deeply, the relations you cheered so much, suddenly shift to one side of the line. There, on the other side stands our self, confused, anxious, weak, and terrified. But that is the price that you pay, just to gamble upon your conviction. You better hope that you win.

I came back to my apartment last night. Meeting everyone that I possibly could, love them at the last moment as much as I could. I met mom. She blessed me for my journey to the sea (which she knew to be a "research project"). Momma had made my favourite apple pie. Maybe I was being too dramatic. But the odds of the team returning back, with a 100% survival rate, were less than 50%. The apple pie tasted heavenly.

My friends were a delight too. None of them knew the seriousness of the dangers associated with my mission. I did not let them find out. I guess it was for the best.

I had a strong team; each one hand-picked for their skills and experience. Samira was a master in Oceanography. Marine life and diving were her life. Her problem-solving skills made her an excellent fit.

Anish was a key element for us. He was an agile diver, a champion depth explorer, therefore well-suited for our mission. Quiet, calm and mature were the words to describe him.

Sonia and I knew each other well before. I first met her during an international summit on preserving the Indian Ocean and its ecosystem. She was a professional cartographer and an expert on Indian Ocean's ecosystem and infrastructure. She was a soft-spoken personality, yet a genius when it came to navigation.

As far as David was concerned, we had a little history together. We will talk about it some other day! David was, however, a resourceful man. From his looks and attitude, nobody could guess that he headed the Australian Institute of Marine Sciences.

It had been nine hours since we boarded the N45 Tambor Class submarine vessel. I was amazed at the condition it was in. Especially for a vessel built in the 1940s.

David had some connections in an American private military company. He managed to borrow the submarine for our journey. And he took a million from his research grant fund.

It was only 350 metres deep beneath the ocean, and the chilling silence surrounded us. I am still fascinated by these magnificent creatures. Living their lives in anonymity, exploring the mysteries of the ocean darks, and making humans awe over them.

We were surfaced for about two hours and moved at 15 knots to cover the distance quickly. But David decided to move slowly, some 90 nautical miles from our target.

"Well! I think a halt would be a better choice. Judging by the vessel's age and Sonar's reading," said Samira. Her blue eyes scanned the vessel, as if assessing its integrity. "We cannot push this thing to its limits. It is too old," she said.

David made brief eye contact with her, impressed by Samira's mechanical prowess. David was checking out the pressure gauges to his right, not willing to halt at all. And I began to see the interaction between the team members as not so desirable.

"40 nautical miles to the drop zone," declared David on the intercom radio. I began sorting my gear too. Wetsuit, dive computer, regulator, cylinder… Suddenly, a sound shook all of us. It was a loud screeching sound, something like what car brakes make; only much louder, bolder and frightening. I sensed danger, and alarms beeped throughout the vessel.

"Put on your survival gear. We'll be fine. Probably hit a reef," instructed David.

The crew panicked. Though the beeping alarms and warning bell stopped after a minute, our hearts stopped pounding only after an hour.

"What was that?" I asked David.

"We hit a reef," he replied.

"Is that normal? I mean, with Submarines?" I asked with serious concern.

"It's fine. The Sonar is working," said David. I told them to check the damage. After all, the blow to the sub was not a little thing.

"We are 10 nautical miles from the target. We will assess the damage once we surface there," David assured me with his calm and composed voice.

"Ready for the first dive yet?" he asked to check our confidence. "Yes! Yes! We are," I said.

I was a restless kid. I never really wanted to wait for anything. That is how kids are – restless and impulsive. They don't really like to delay things. "Learn to be patient, Donna," my mom always advised me. This was one of her lessons that stuck with me. These lines remained with me forever. *"Delay is always better than distress."* Wise. Protective. I came to realize this teaching in my adulthood. Delaying something you really want is always better than an uncalled for trouble. If the circumstances do not allow you, it is simple – you should wait.

David miscalculated the situation and the submarine hit something. No more risk taking if we all want to come out alive. I became surer of my conviction, Delay is always better than distress. Overconfidence will diminish our chances of survival.

Day 2

"Victory loves preparation..."

Anish and I put on the gear. Wetsuit, mask, oxygen tanks, auxiliary tanks, regulators, GPS, radio, headlights, and live-cam feed. We cross-checked each other's gear and device fittings, twice... thrice. We were ready to investigate the possible damage to our vessel. Now, it might seem easy for an outsider to watch us dive. With all the equipments and training, deep diving might seem like a sport. But it's not! It is far from a sport, even far from a safe activity. A slight slip of luck and things can go haywire. There are no second chances.

We were already more than 350 metres below the ocean surface. The submarine's pressure-controlled cabins kept us in comfort. Though, outside lay an unforgiving aquatic world. Imagine 350 metres of water above your head. Such amount of water is enough to dissolve gases in the liquids. Yet, Anish and I moved to a ballast-chamber in the lower deck. "Stay safe mates," David radioed in. I turned the heavy vault-door lock. Both of us rushed in and locked the chamber door from inside manually.

We put on the masks and waited for the green light signal. Once the green light showed up, the chamber began flooding with the water. This was the standard way of diving from a submarine. Once the chamber filled up with water, the exterior door opened towards the vast, infinite ocean.

"There is only one rule to survive down there," Mr A. Pawar's voice stuck me. "Never lose control. Never lose hope until you've hit the bottom." I was a trainee diving cadet during the Trans-Antarctic Oceanic expedition. Mr Pawar was the Maritime Department Head, and I was one of his most enthusiastic students. I remember how during a dive, my oxygen tank malfunctioned. I was 20-25 metres deep. I started gasping for air. My equipment was heavy. I tried kicking my legs to flutter as hard as possible. The harder I fluttered, the darker my vision got. I tried shouting, but in vain. I accepted that I was meant to die like this. I lost control and started descending into the ocean. I remember a faint light hitting my face. I was being surfaced by my fellow divers. One of them was my Maritime Department Head. A day's treatment and hot coffee with the sailors helped me regain my senses. Though, the incident taught me a crucial lesson. 'Victory loves preparation. One can never lose control.'

As we carried our weightless bodies out of the ballast chamber gate, we entered into a surreal world – dark blue, shimmering, deep, infinite, cold, mysterious, and moaning. Such was the character of the waters we had dived into. Our flashlights shined like the bright rays in a universe where light was a rarity. "Beautiful, isn't it?" Anish was awed with what we were going through.

"Never been so deep before?" I asked him.

"200, yes. 350, no!" he replied.

"Donna, do you hear me?" Sonia radioed in.

"We hear you," I replied back. "We are heading towards the place of impact," I said to Sonia and signalled Anish.

Samira and David were monitoring the mission closely. Samira constantly evaluated the equipment's performance while David was in charge of submarine operations. Sonia became our eyes in the ocean. She was responsible for navigating us to the point of impact. "This is how astronauts must feel like in the space station?" Anish was fascinated.

"I bet so," I replied.

We cycled our feet slowly towards the nose of the submarine. Our breath could be heard over the radio signal.

Meanwhile, Samira also worked out if we could move closer to the north point of the Kola Regio. That place was roaring deep. Terrible weather, unstable water, and extreme depth. But that point was our best bet to get started with the treasure hunt. We were closing in on the point. The pressure of the water was immense. At one point, I could literally hear bells ringing in my ears. I figured it was due to megatons of hydrostatic pressure. Very few small fishes were visible at this depth. Low light and cold water favour nobody.

"Don't let the strangeness and silence distract you," M. Pawar instructed his team. "You lose focus, you lose mental balance. At such depths, attention is your best hope," I remembered his voice.

"We are at the impact site," I radioed into the control room.

"Please focus your flashlight and cams towards the impacted area," said David. Both of us did the same. At the impact-site were two large dents. The metal was strongly impacted, but thankfully no leakages were detected.

"Can you run me a bit closer towards that steel plate?" David requested Anish, who pointed his camera towards the plate. The plate had a massive dent near the bolts.

"How much time to fix it?" asked Samira.

"Will take three hours approx," he said.

"Go ahead!" she radioed in.

"But we need to prepare the welding arc and gather some tools. We will be able to initiate the repairs after a few hours. Get the team assembled. We have to fix the repairs before sunlight, precious time!" David advised the crew.

I began mapping the next few hours. I hoped for things to fall into place.

Day 3

"Making ends meet..."

"How do we repair this?" asked Anish.

"We'll do the welding from the inside," replied Samira. Still floating weightless outside the submarine with me, I signalled him to return to the submarine.

"We're returning. Vessel diagnosis is complete." I radioed.

We would have barely swum 15 feet or so when Anish stopped abruptly, glancing at something. I was behind him and tried to look in the direction he was looking in.

"Anish! What is it?" I radioed him. He seemed too busy to notice my voice. "Anish!" I repeated over the mouthpiece, still trying to look where he was looking. We were looking at something at our own depth level, probably 40 to 50 feet away from us. Anish raised his right hand and clenched his fist (signaling me to freeze and remain alert). That gesture scared me, to be honest.

The reason for our motionless limbs and awe-struck eyes was apparent a few seconds later. There it was! A giant shadow, as heavy as a ship, with a slow movement. There it was, a few feet away from us, nature's magnificence itself – the giant blue whale.

She was cutting through the depth with her little calf, big enough to crush us to death, probably moving towards the south side of the ocean, hundreds of miles from here. It was simply majestic.

"Gosh! Did you see that?" Anish's excitement was all over the radio.

"Yes, we did. Did you both see it?" asked Sonia with a tone of excitement.

"Yes, our first magic moment." I was lost for the next few minutes, trying to absorb what I had just witnessed.

The airlock chamber opened with some effort as the pressure difference was a bit irregular. The chamber flooded again, we entered inside it, and the compartment pressurized again pushing the water outside. Anish and I removed our heavy diving gear and went up straight to the upper deck. The crew welcomed us with a brief smile and Sonia gave us a report on the mission.

"David is preparing for welding. Samira is helping him out. We should be fine with a good weld," said Sonia.

I was relieved for the moment. However, not for once forgetting the danger that lay ahead. Anish went to the topmost deck to change. I was feeling hungry and headed to the middle deck level.

"We have a problem here," David declared on the intercom. "This needs immediate attention." My heart surged with the negative anticipation. It always goes the same way. You think for a moment, the worst possibility, and… it manifests.

We all rushed through the narrow chambers of the vessel towards the meeting point. The scene shocked all of us. Right below the dent site was a small leakage. The water was pouring in with a high-pressure jet stream. The compartment had about two feet of flood inside of it. "Not good! Not good!" murmured David. Caution alarms beeped, lighting the chamber red intermittently.

"Shouldn't we surface?" asked Samira.

"No. We need to fix it fast. Surfacing will increase the jet pressure. Also, the crack is increasing in size, if you may have noticed!" David said.

"Where is Anish?" asked Sonia with obvious worry in her tone.

"On the upper deck," I said.

We were in a trouble much deeper than we had originally thought. "How much time to fix the weld?" I asked David and Samira.

"Two hours. But we have another problem as well," said David.

"What?" I asked.

"The welding gas cylinder is not enough to repair a large weld. We need extra oxygen," he said, turning his head towards the oxygen cylinders hung up in the chamber.

"Are you sure we cannot pull this off any other way?" I was shocked. "Our diving attempts will become limited; we might even lose our auxiliary oxygen." I found myself in an obvious dilemma. Using up auxiliary oxygen meant losing diving time, compromising the mission's success. We, obviously, couldn't let the vessel bleed the water in.

Without the submarine, the mission would not have continued. This was a risk I had to take. No other options. "Let's do it then," I said.

"Oceans and deserts are unforgiving. You'll sometimes have to make difficult choices. With difficult decisions comes the ability to reap fortunes," Mr Pawar had once said to me.

My mom Katherine raised three children on her own, despite the hardships my father created. My mom gradually became my hero. She always used to say, "As in life, as in death, you'll always have to make ends meet."

Day 4

"You either chase dreams, or they haunt you back."

The mind works in weird ways. Your aspirations, dreams, goals and missions are deeply embedded within yourself. You belong to them, they belong to you. Though, if you become desperate, leave any of them untouched, stop in either of them, they come to haunt you. Haunting dreams take away the will power, enforce fear of failure and breed laziness in the person. Such a person, you shall not become. I learned this lesson after many failures. And, even today, I am not sure of the success, even survival. Such is our mind. Such is our weird mind.

"Two hours and 320 cubic feet of oxygen," Samira murmured as she walked past me from the gallery. I wanted an estimate of how much resources would be consumed during the repair. 320 cubic feet of oxygen meant an hour of additional time under the water for the mission. We just lost it! Lost oxygen meant lesser mission time. We were running pretty tight on time and resources, for we had already started with a negative road map.

"Guys! We are running two hours behind the schedule. Dive oxygen is four cylinders short. Keep the limits of our mission in mind." As I spoke, the crew stared at each other to comprehend the seriousness of the situation. They knew it already. My words just got them thinking. Samira returned to the navigation room with Sonia. David was in the engine room, giving the vessel's power plant another check.

I went back to upper deck; the small round glass window was what I loved the most. I could see the vast, endless ocean from it. The glass often showed me a partial reflection of myself, as if I was in the water. "Fascinating!"

My personal belongings contained clothes, maps, medical kit, fifty-six-year old whisky and the pictures of those I loved. I held the old-scotch by its fine glass neck. Turned it and read its label. *Finest Scotch for Finest Moments.* What a relief that label was to me.

"Guys! This is Donna. Please come at the main deck," I called for a mission meeting."

Within two minutes, everyone was present on the deck, except for David. "Where is David?" asked Sonia after noticing his absence.

"Anish, radio him in," I said, but no reply.

I decided to carry on without him. We all gathered around a table. I spread the ocean map over it. "Samira, how is the vessel doing?" I asked.

"We are doing 7 knots an hour. Let's say 60% of the engine capacity, and we will be fine," she explained.

"Makes sense," Anish supported Samira's opinion.

"Okay, how much time to the target?" I asked Sonia.

She looked a little sleepy. She removed her glasses with one hand, and refreshed her right eye by rubbing it with the other. "Assuming the same speed and direction, we will reach the target by tomorrow same time," said Sonia, putting her spectacles back.

I took a few slow steps to look out of the window. Pitch black. Haunting. "10:15 p.m.?" I asked.

"Hopefully!!" Sonia replied.

I couldn't wait but formulate a plan for the time we reached our destination. "Alright!" I clicked my fingers while walking back to the table. "Here is the plan for when we touch the Blue Hole," I said. "Three divers will exit the submarine at once. Two explorers, and one probee. Probee will follow the explorers to keep an eye on the surroundings and explorers' equipments." The crew went on listening, critically evaluating every word.

"Our first checkpoint will be the base of the Blue Hole. Let's check the lighting instruments before we go to sleep," I advised.

I, however, wondered about David. It was strange. He was still missing. This was a mission meeting. How could he be not present here? I was confused about his behaviour. "We will discuss the details once we touch the destination," I said as I dismissed the meeting. Everyone went back to what they were doing.

I was worried about the mission. Was this crazy? Would it be fatal…of course! My thoughts bombarded my forehead as I stepped into the narrow gallery to look for David. He must be on the upper deck, I thought. The submarine had become quiet by now. Samira will pilot this vessel all night, before the next shift-change.

"David! David!" I yelled as I neared the deck.

Day 5

"Stay high, fly high..."

It was 10:35 p.m. My diver's watch was as reliable as my memory. I could see a room door partially open, with light beaming the narrow gallery. Old English music played inside the room. I opened the door wide as I stepped in without knocking.

"Hey!" I called to David.

No sign of him in the room. The room was filled with a smoky smell. I got closer to the washroom. As I entered, I noticed the bathroom had tons of smoke. Cigarette!

There stood the man. Holding a burning cigarette in one hand, covering his mouth with the other while coughing.

"Hey, Donna! How you doing?" David said as I inspected every inch of it.

"What is wrong with you?" I was deeply annoyed and frustrated at his actions.

"You've got your way to focus on a mission; I've I got mine," he said with his signature evil smile.

"Gosh, David!" I was on the verge of breakdown. "Our mission was delayed. The vessel got hit. Oxygen stacks were depleted. The team needs support. And here you are, an experienced and knowledgeable man, smoking, bunking the mission meeting." I felt like punching him in the face. *I know you want to hit me,* the English country song continued to play in the background.

"You know, you've got problem. A big one," he said, leaning back on the wall, looking up while smoking. "You want to conquer it all; the mission is all about you. Yes, the treasure will be the greatest discovery. But you've got to keep it cool." I couldn't believe he held that opinion of me. But surprisingly, I was listening to him.

"What do you want to say, David?" I asked him in a serious tone.

"Look! I am on this mission for a treasure hunt. But I've got nothing to lose," he said. "The best accomplishments by humans were possible, not because they were serious, but because they knew how to celebrate the moments as they came."

I gave a dead stare into his eyes, obviously shook deeply by his words.

"What do you mean, David?" I asked, again.

"What are the odds that we will reach the treasure?" he asked. "Let's discuss here. What are the chances that we will find the treasure?" David asked again.

"Look… if everything goes as planned, we can get what we want. You are an experienced person, David. Why am I explaining this to you?" As I questioned, he put the burning cigarette in his mouth and took a big puff.

"You still don't get it Donna," he replied.

"What is this all about David, seriously? You're getting on my nerves." I was losing my patience.

Then, as he released the damned smoke like dragon fire, still looking at me with sleepy eyes, he said, "The probability of us returning alive from the Blue Hole is less than half. Hey! I am good in maths, Donna." He shrugged while making his point, "I have been noticing that you are too serious…. and… *desperate* to reach your goal." I was constantly looking at him with raised brows as he went on. "The Universe loves making things harder when you're desperate. Stop being one!" He said while smoking continuously.

I exhaled slowly, and was confused thinking if he was right. No. He was high. But his observations are keen and powerful. What if…I am becoming restless?' I began having doubts on my strongest convictions. The room was full of smoke, David was staring at me, for the briefest moment. I was transported into the harrowing depths of my memories.

"What is this Donna?" Senior diver Rubin pointed at me. Being a girl was unacceptable in this tough world.

"Bronze diving medal, master," I said loudly. I looked straight, head up, and all attentive.

"Throw that away, Donna! You are never gonna dive again. I want you to live in the city with all the comforts. I want you to get engaged, married and raise children. But not diving. Is that clear?" Master Rubin yelled at me with all authority.

That moment… Those words… Seven years ago. Was that the reason for my 'desperation'? I have dived since then. My instructor had advised me to give up diving… forever. Today,

I was captaining this vessel, this submarine, with a skilled crew to search for one of the biggest ever treasure. I need time off. I need space to think. I need to relax, I thought. I pulled out my radio, and decided to check once in the engine room. "Samira, do you hear me, over?"

"I thought you were asleep Donna," she said slightly surprised.

"Almost asleep," I radioed back. "I'll be there to take over in the morning," I said as I cut the chat. David was still staring at me, probably lost in his thoughts. "Give me that!" I walked up to him and took the cigarette away.

Three large puffs and it was just like old times. Here I was smoking-up with an old friend, 400 metres under the sea, in a damaged submarine. As I released the smoke, and cleared all the toxins with a slow mind, I gazed upwards at the ceiling. I could visualize the plan. "David… you're good." I patted him on the back.

"I know," he said. I let my doubt fly away with it. Morning was the time for us to be in action.

"Good night, David," I said as I exited the upper deck.

"Good night, Donna," he wished back. That was one move that made me believe in myself. Live a little, and let go a little. I went to the small round window, and looked outside. I could just see a light beam blending into the dark night.

"I am coming for you," I promised the depths as I prepared for the sleep.

Day 6

"If you are restless, you might already be in the battleground."

It was probably a lovely morning; 'probably' because we couldn't see the sunlight reaching that depth. We were away from any known traces of a civilized society. We were away from any help. We were alone. The vessel looked like a house bustling with morning chores of a family of five. Someone just woke up; someone prepared the coffee, while early risers were checking the equipment. Felt like the crew's spirit was braver than mine.

"Here is a soft, buttery French omelette," Sonia hurried inside the meeting room and put up a white ceramic plate in front of me.

The omelette was indeed caramelized with butter. "Wow! Smells lovely, just like you, Sonia." I said as soon as I crunched the breakfast.

"Military Service Group did us a favour by lending this mighty vessel," Samira remarked as she strolled into the meeting room with her coffee.

"Not really, a commission also awaits them if we are successful, but they are not counting on it much." I said to her.

I rushed straight to the control room. My feet were swift, sure, and strong.

"How much time to the target?" I asked Anish.

He looked like he hadn't slept last night, "Eleven hours to the destination!" He replied firmly. The submarine was piercing the ice-cold water with 12 knots.

I went back to the meeting room. Except for Anish, everyone assembled there.

"Guys! The moment is only few hours away." I could sense thrill, excitement, terror – all together. The team felt the same way. I could see it in their eyes. "We will soon touch the Sentinel island. Once I conclude the session, each crew member is supposed to check the equipment. Watch each other's back at all times. Bring the treasure, help each other out." I was all ready for the action. The crew clapped. There were smiles I could see. David looked tired.

"I won't discuss the details of our plan. We all are united by our skills, and the hunger to make that treasure ours. Get your equipment, get all the essentials. We all will meet within an hour to formulate the first dive strategy."

I could feel, and almost hear the depths getting bigger and mysterious. We were in the battleground now. I had waited for this moment my entire life. My face blushed at this thought.

We spent the afternoon working on our equipment, mapping the sea, communicating and coordinating. Kola Regio, that no diver had yet conquered, was only a few hours away. The crew was focusing on equipment functionality, survival gear, and dive techniques to assist each other. The more we could minimize the risk of such a hostile environment, the probability of us hitting the treasure would shoot up dramatically. The afternoon went well. We were finally relaxed, almost ready for the mission.

9:45 p.m.

"Teams! Buckle up. All units take up your position…" before I could end my sentence, Samira spoke up.

"Are we in trouble?" said Samira.

"We are actually going to have to cross a narrow gorge. We have an option to reroute our mission. But it will increase our destination point by a hundred miles. That means a delay of another fifteen hours," said David.

"How risky is the gorge?" asked Sonia.

"Gorge is pretty risky. The vessel is already damaged. Would it be safe?" he questioned.

I somehow anticipated that I wasn't far away from a difficult question, the sort that puts you into a stressful dilemma.

"A gorge?" I was actually surprised. How come we did not see it on the map? I needed an answer from the experts.

"These maps are old. I bet no cartographer ever thought of bringing a submarine out here and decided to measure the depths," replied Sonia.

Our risk just increased. "How come we did not see this coming?" I asked as I began scrutinizing the whole situation. "This does not look good," I said. Then David put on his serious face. I recognized this face when he ran out of solutions to a problem. I never wanted him to make that face, but in vain.

"I guess we need to think this one through. A hundred extra miles means more fuel for the vessel, and decreased time. But, if we take the submarine through the gorge, our risk of damaging it increases. Though, we save time and fuel in return," said David, spilling his best options before us.

"If we risk it all to save some time and fuel, we might not even reach the destination, lest we damage this craft. This is a pretty sophisticated and old vessel. We can keep it intact at the expense of some time and fuel. We can then compensate with our dive times," said Samira.

"Sonia!" I asked her for her opinion again.

"I think we should follow the experts. Samira seems to be right!" replied Sonia.

One look at David's face revealed he was someone who would never trade risk to save time.

It was 10:30 p.m. I decided to make a radio announcement. We had to change the course. This vessel was a mode of our survival. It would keep us safe. I had learnt long ago in a management course to take long-term decisions carefully. Haste leads to distress. "Calling all units… N45 will now change its course. Our destination is due for another fifteen hours."

David and I were supposed to pilot it tonight. The crew needed rest. A good sleep would make them better. It was at that moment when Samira abruptly stopped as we all dismissed ourselves. She came back to the table and said, "Maybe, maybe we can pull this one off." Her words stuck my brain at once. I was too eager to know how, as we were so close to the mission point. "Maybe if two divers assist the vessel out of the gorge, we can take it slowly, without taking any hits. A little coordination will do the trick!" she said.

David and I listened carefully. It made sense.

"What's the plan?" asked David.

"If we prepare the crew and take the vessel through the gorge, it is almost eight miles of narrow pathway," said Samira. I visualized the events in my mind.

"We can do it now, then!" I was feeling the same rush again. "So here is the plan! By 12:30 a.m, we all gather at this point. Your equipment and devices are all top-notch. We are touching the waters of death tonight!" I said as I looked outside the round glass window.

Day 7

"Keep moving forward..."

I was a little surprised by David's look. He earlier favoured to take the vessel through the gorge, but now seemed disappointed by the idea. He was senior to me. I never questioned him. But I was puzzled. What does he want? Is he judging us? Is this an impulsive decision? I kept thinking. Then again, the mission was near. I had to prepare.

Everyone was present in the mission control room by 12:00 a.m. I could notice the excitement in their eyes. A few were skeptical too.

"Are we sure about doing this?" Sonia asked to check if everyone was on the same page.

"Yeah!" Anish cheered.

I was about to unravel the plan before them. "Sonia, I and Anish will go outside and assist in navigation. For every 200 metres forward, we will check the pathway. David and Samira will keep an eye on us from the inside. David, you'll check the vessel's health at all times," I instructed. "If we coordinate well, we can be on the other side within forty minutes."

"Yeah!!!" The team cheered together, as they always did. All of us rushed to our respective spots.

"Time to meet the floodgates again," said Anish.

"Sonia, you all right?" Anish asked her.

"I am all set. Check my regulator once though," she said while putting on the equipment harness.

"Sure." Anish went on to help her.

"Guys! Dive chamber in five minutes," I instructed them.

The site inside the vessel had suddenly changed. We all were supposed to either sleep or keep the submarine on course. Now we were all working together to push it through a narrow gorge underneath the water. The gorge was the only way now to maintain depth and reach as close as possible to the target location.

The navigation team was in position. My radio then suddenly popped a message from David. "One of you, take a harpoon with you. You don't know when you'll meet a wild species," said David.

"Ok David," I replied. I was carrying the metal harpoon, used to kill whales. It was a powerful weapon. I was just hoping for a situation when I don't have to use it. I, Anish and Sonia gathered in the airlock again. It was Sonia's first mission dive; she was trying to maintain the cool she was known for.

The three of us put on the masks, double-checked our regulators and communication equipment. "Ready?" radioed in Samira.

"Yeah," said Anish as Sonia and I gave him thumbs up. The chamber began flooding rapidly again as the airlock opened up. The water pressure was hundreds of times greater than the air.

In no time, we found ourselves out in the ocean. Our headlamps were the only way we could see through the waters. The vessel's front light lit up the forward path, and rear part also lit up dimly.

"It is going to be rigorous," I warned them. We were floating freely with our fins and underwater scooters.

"Probe team! All okay?" asked David from inside the control room.

"Yeah! Anish will keep an eye on the rear part of the submarine. I and Sonia are reaching for the front. Darkness is making this tougher than it is," I said as I swam forward, slowly and steadily.

Sonia and I checked the next 200 metres or so.

"All clear," she announced on the radio. "Bring the sub forward," said Sonia.

We kept crawling forward and assisted the sub at every metre. We could hear the engine humming silently, spinning the propeller at a minimum speed. The submarine glided slowly through the gorge, David piloting it carefully. We could not risk even a few inches as it would have damaged the vessel. Anish swam along the rear stabilizing fin of the submarine while keeping an eye on the situation from the back. As I whirled my body in front of the sub lights, I could feel a strange rush inside my head. It was the anticipation of what was coming. I was closer to my goal than ever before.

At one point, I thought the treasure was pulling us towards it, compelling us to take impulsive decisions. Within the next fifty minutes, N45 was standing on the other side of the gorge.

Day 8

"Of their own accord..."

For a minute the radios echoed with the chatter of claps and cheers. "Whoohoo!" "Hoo-ya!" "Yes! We did it," went into my ears together. I was happy. Not just because we had crossed a barrier, but because this was the first real teamwork undertaken by the crew. "Bravo! Guys, here we are." I radioed in everyone.

A mesmerizing scene awaited us. Sonia, I and Anish dropped our jaws at what stood in front of us – the enormous, gigantic, deep, dark blue ocean. The deep-sea valley threw us into oblivion by its sheer magnificence. For a brief moment, my soul wandered off into the far ventures of the unexplored ocean. "It... is... beautiful!!" Sonia was awed by the whole scene.

"I have never seen anything like this before. Guys! Can you see what we see?" radioed Anish, still unable to believe his eyes.

I was sure that I could sense the sea floor all along while crossing the gorge. As soon as the vessel crossed it, I encountered the strangest sensation. The sea floor suddenly vanished. I felt like there was an infinite depth beneath me. We were only 400 metres deep back there. My echo-sounder indicated 2955 metres of water level beneath our current standing.

"Time for some sea-walking. Anish, Sonia, you go 200 metres right, I will explore the forward position. The ocean life at this depth is no less than a treasure in itself." I adjusted my light as I moved ahead.

I swam to about 90 feet in the north direction with steady paddling. Air bubbles passed beside me, rising up to the surface, which was about 3500 metres above my head. I turned back and saw the Tambor's lights. At this depth, the vessel was slowly fading away into a shadow, appearing as a giant ghostly specter shortly after. At another 300 feet, I lost visual contact with Anish and Sonia. "Visual contact lost," I alerted the divers.

"Yes Donna," both of them replied in sync. We were not looking for anything. It was just an exploratory dive. 'Probably, I should look for a place to commence the mission. We need a starting point,' I thought.

"Sonia! How far is the sea floor?" I asked her over the radio.

"Its a steep drop as far as my Sonar reads. 1500 metres drop for the next 20 kilometres or so," she replied with affirmative calculations.

"Can you give me the terrain report?" I asked her.

"I'll have to map it back in the submarine. I won't be able to tell because of the visibility," said Sonia.

"Okay then! Anish, Sonia, let's get back into the vessel. The treasure hunt is on, and we have a lot of work to do." I radioed the divers, tracing back my path towards the vessel.

Day 9

"Watch out! Don't get killed."

It was 4:25 a.m. and nobody really went to sleep. Excitement and thrill of being so close to the goal had enthralled the will to rest. I woke up, removed my blanket, felt the positive vibes across my feet, and set the foot on the floor with a smile. I got up, retrospecting last night's brief exploratory dive, and moved towards the window. Same fascinating universe outside, I thought.

I put on my green top and khaki cargos. My watch, radio, and I were ready for the day. I moved out into the corridor. As I neared the mission room, I patted Sonia's back as she stood with a coffee mug in her hand. She greeted me with a sweet smile. I reached for the table and removed the clutter (maps, and papers). "Folks! Meeting time it is." I announced in a rather sleepy voice.

Anish looked at me with a smile while he fixed one of the oxygen cylinders. David walked into the room with a cigarette in his mouth. "What's up people! Anyone hungry for the omelette?" he asked in a loud tone.

"I'll have some," I said. He offered me the buttery soft omelette and I prepared for the meeting.

"We have touched the site. Bravo work last night!" The crew self-cheered as I spoke those words. "We are now beginning with the mission." Everyone had gathered around the table by that time.

"Let's start by getting real-time situational awareness. Be ready with what you all have." I instructed them all. I looked at David and prompt him to start.

"Well, the submarine took some hits, but looks good as of now. We can dive no further. We are already at the "crush depth" of the vessel." His words shook me.

"What do you mean crush depth?"

"Well, this vessel is made up of HY-80 steel. I have been registering bends and structural pressure since we crossed the gorge. We will have to resurface. We can only carry deep diving from a maximum depth of 550 metres below the sea-level." David went on. The crew's excitement vanished, and stress suddenly appeared on the forehead.

"You mean to say we've been risking it all along?" Samira asked in a tone of concern. "Well, then take us to the surface, we can carry on the meeting from there," said Samira without even reacting mildly to the seriousness of the situation.

"Let's move, move, move everyone," I shouted and within a moment, the crew dispersed into their respective places. "We need to surface, and change our dive strategy."

"David, come with me! We need to talk." I held him back as others focused on their tasks. "What is happening? I thought we were about to dive," I said.

"I did try my best to keep the vessel intact. There is only so much the steel can take," David said.

"We will have to change our whole diving strategy. You know that, right?" I expressed my concerns in a rather serious tone. David did not seem to bother.

"So… we're improvising. True adventurers always improvise, dear!" he said.

"Touching the seabed with limited oxygen is a risk, and you know that, David!"

"I know many things, Donna! Diving is one of them. I just don't know what Samira is up to. Didn't she notice the fact that we were below the threshold limit for this vessel?" He stated in a monotonous tone. "I am just surprised you did not notice her behaviour. She has lost focus since we hit the submarine in that reef. Samira should have alerted us."

David's words got me thinking. He was right. All this time we were living under a serious threat. 'Now those crackling sounds make sense. It was the steel under immense pressure,' I thought.

"Let's surface then! We all need a serious talk," I said to him as I walked away to look for the map.

Twenty minutes out and we surfaced above the water, making an enormous up splash like that of a whale. We hadn't seen light for a long time now. Somewhere, deep down in our hearts, we were relieved to connect with the outer world where we belonged.

It was 5:30 a.m. The sun was up with its warmth, the ocean was calm. I thought the crew would like some fresh air, so I asked Anish to open the deck hatch. Within no time, we all were out.

"Enjoy the day while you all can. We need to discuss the 'incident' that just happened. We have to renew our mission strategy," I said as I tracked a seagull fly-by over the blue waters.

"Refresh yourselves with the sights of real world. It is going to be tough from tomorrow on," David said surprisingly, when nobody expected!

Day 10

"Falls make you climb higher, higher and higher."

Next morning was a still, calm and peaceful one. N45 stood still on the waters. Last night, demotivation and terror had shaken us. We were playing under a risk that could not be afforded. David revealed the threat too late. Samira missed the threat altogether. I stood at the open deck as the ocean breeze blew my hair.

David came up the deck looking for me. I glanced at him and went back to tracing the far reaches of the ocean where it touched the horizon. "How are you"? he asked in a lowered voice. I sensed that he was feeling apologetic, and somehow guilty for bringing everyone to the risk.

"Fine," I said while continuing to look at the horizon. "How long have you been familiar with the submarines, David?" I asked him.

"All my life... I met the first metal beast when I was twelve. My father was a sailor in the Irish navy." He replied as his hands searched for something in his pant pockets.

"You didn't know about the high risk of structural failure? How come you suddenly realised it last morning?" I wanted to know.

"It was a calculated risk, Donna," he said nonchalantly.

"Did you take any consensus with the crew? Did you inform them? No! You risked all our lives because of a non-productive and utterly stupid risk, David." I was beginning to lose it. "How long have you been with the Navy?" I inquired.

"Eight long years."

"Why did you become a mercenary, David?" I asked.

"No reason. Money maybe!" He replied in a slightly defensive tone.

"Still… Nobody leaves the Navy without a reason. Were you court-martialed? Be honest here…" I tried to dig deeper with an assertive tone. There was a brief moment of silence. Only the waves and the seagulls far away in the background were restless.

"Does it make a difference? Are you questioning my integrity here, Donna?" David got strangely defensive.

"Maybe! It is important to know the people I am working with. Our success is dependent on our lives… if we make it out alive…" I said.

David was silent. "Well, I don't think you should know the things that you don't want to," he said as he turned around and went back inside the hatch. That was the moment I realized everything was not right with the team. There was something that David was hiding, and I had to know what it was.

I walked back, and climbed down into the lower deck. There was a creepy yet peaceful silence inside the vessel. Some people were resting. Some others were busy. I decided to keep David aside for a while, and focus on the new diving strategy.

Anish was reading *Moby Dick* sitting in the corner bunk of the mission room. "Hey Anish! Can you gather the crew? Found something worthy in that book? Haha!" I poked him. Anish closed the book with a clap, put it aside, and stood up.

"Crew! Urgent meeting aboard. Mission room, now," Anish commanded over the radio. Within no time, Samira, Sonia, Anish, I and David found ourselves in the mission room that smelt like salt water. David's masculine, hunky body overshadowed the small elements around him. He was the kind of man I could rely on for commanding and directing the crew. Though, I always failed to understand his ways. Strangely calm, David seemed to be in deep thought.

"We are all, I guess, aware of the situation. There is going to be a slight change in our mission schedule," said David while checking out his watch. "I have formulated a dive strategy for us. We cannot take the N45 below 200 metres from now on. It is going to be a challenging dive every time. Our oxygen will be utilized faster, which means we will have way less time per dive than expected. At this point, the mission is a do or die. Anyone who wants to exit can walk away now, no harsh feelings. But, if you decide to stay, make sure you play by the rules, and keep other lives equal to yours." David displayed a magnificent sense of authority when I almost got puzzled by the situation.

"Of course, you have many questions. We need to be a team first, and accountants for our actions later. Submarine's structure cannot be stressed further. We have depleted more than 15% of oxygen that was to be used for diving. If the treasure really belongs to us, these resources will be sufficient enough to get us through." As David went on, the crew got more and more entangled by his words.

"We will schedule the diving after midnight as Sonia forecasts the water to be stable at that time," he said. "Enjoy the day while we are surfaced. Relax, and rest. Try to breed trust if you can."

Everyone nodded in agreement. Trust, had been breached somewhere deep down between all of us. Though, I was feeling a little in control of the situation. David did it for me.

"As the clock strikes 12, we shall begin exploring the deep waters of the sentinels, and keep moving forward with our vessel."

Day 11

"Let's do it!"

It was our eleventh day at sea. Last night, David's words pumped up the crew, a little. My motivation rekindled. N45 was still surfaced and we changed our dive strategy. I woke up, rubbed my eyes, put on my sleepers and the wristwatch, and went straight to the mission room. Apparently, the crew seemed to be waiting for me. I had slept like a baby for a few hours. It was 12:30 a.m, thirty minutes past midnight. Nobody woke me up so that I could get some rest.

"Hey there, sleepy head! Here, we are getting started," said Sonia as she greeted me with a smile and put her echolocation earpiece on.

"Terrific!" I said. I rushed to get myself a cup of coffee without even greeting others in the mission room. I was simply excited that the diving sessions were actually starting. I headed back to the crew swiftly, switching on my radio as I neared the room. As my eyes got the vision of mission room's entrance, David and I made eye contact and he signalled me to come over.

"Donna! Sonia and Samira are preparing for the dive. Get your gear. You are exploring the rock caverns at 1500 metres. Here, take this sensor," said David.

"Is this the C42?" I asked taking the gadget in my hand and inspecting it with keen eyes.

"Yeah! Just place it onto a rock and we'd be able to trace metal presence nearby. Also, it'll make it easier for us to not look for the same area again!" said David.

I went to the deck to collect my essentials. Finally, the day has come. I collected my goggles, my fins, and the shoulder light. 'Time to go, Donna. Waters are calling.' The thought kept ringing in my head.

"Divers. Assemble at the deck. Assemble at the deck," David chattered over the radio. I rushed out to the deck.

Sonia and Samira were all geared up. The all-women crew was marking the beginning of a journey whose end nobody had the faintest idea of. Anish and David were in charge of communications and navigation.

I stood at the bridge of the vessel. The waves made a soothing sound, and so did the wind. I could hear myself breathing with my ears covered in the dive-suit. Occasional radio noise somehow kept me from fading away into thoughts. Sonia, Samira and I jumped into the cold deep blue waters. The splash created bubble froth, and within a second, the outer world vanished. I found myself under the magnificent layers of the Sentinel waters. Breathing sounds became louder, and large air bubbles rushed upwards as I descended into the chilly ocean.

I slowly turned around, still descending, trying to gain situational awareness. The water had fair visibility.

"Radio check, comin' in," Anish established the first communication from the vessel.

"Donna here!" Then came another voice, "Samira here," and then "Sonia." I immediately swam towards the duo as we descended to 180 metres. David and Anish were supposed to guide us from the vessel to locate a specific point that was 1500 metres below. For the moment, I enjoyed my weightless body as it got closer to the ocean floor.

"You three probably do not remember the map. So, we will guide you. Follow the instructions closely. You should reach rally point Alpha in about forty minutes!" David said. "Keep an eye on your barometre. Check in again when you reach 300 metres."

"Got that," I replied to David. I turned back as I felt a presence behind my back. Nothing. I scanned the farthest point I could, but spotted nothing. No movement at all. Just a few silver fish here and there. A loud thud on my back and severe water disturbance shook me, and I turned around to a horror.

Sonia was fading away fast. Her hands stretched towards us as she moved towards the darkest lengths of the Sentinel waters. Something was dragging her away with mighty force. I gauged the whole situation as I came back to my senses. Samira was in shock. I tapped her shoulder and took out the loaded harpoon.

"What is happening?" David and Anish shouted over the radio. I had no time to reply. I shot the harpoon just above Sonia's head. A slight red mist was seen in the water and Sonia stopped abruptly. She began descending into the deep, but that was not the matter of concern.

The matter of concern was the monstrous great white shark coming towards us. As it took a U-turn, in an attempt to catch its falling prey, I loaded another arrow into the harpoon, this time with an intention to end it all. As the shark sped towards Sonia, I triggered the metal arrow under tension, and the shark was more of a dead one by that time. The harpoon pierced through the beast, killing it after a little struggle. "This is an emergency," I radioed the crew.

Anish soon arrived on a small inflatable motorboat. Sonia was too heavy for us to carry to the sub with her equipment. We did not know the intensity of her wounds until Anish lifted her frail body onto the motor boat. I pushed Samira onto the boat. Anish and Samira dragged me in. Poor Sonia lay there unconscious. Her right thigh was bleeding profusely. She could barely speak. I later found out shark's teeth embedded inside her right leg bone.

Our adventure had lasted ten minutes. And, I had already given up any hope to proceed with the mission ever again.

Day 12

"Stay frosty..."

A loud thud made me open up my eyes. As my vision regained focus, at once I became conscious of what had fallen upon us. I looked around and saw nobody. Distant voices and echoes grabbed my attention to the next room.

"This does not look good. She has been bleeding continuously. We need to get her out," David suggested in a serious voice. My heartbeat grew faster. I remembered last night now. Memories kept haunting me. We got Sonia aboard the vessel. Upon inspection, we found several shark teeth embedded in her inner thigh, and right hip. Samira and David took three hours to pluck each of them out. Sonia had not regained consciousness until then.

Anish and I assisted them as David and Samira had some medical training, and had operated on a few animals before; though this was a human. "We need to stop the bleeding. I just hope that her femoral artery is intact," David said. This was the condition a few hours before.

"Hey! How's she doing now?" I asked Samira.

"Not good! She woke up for a few minutes last night, hasn't moved since then. Pulse is low. I just hope she makes it through." Samira's words sent a spine-chilling wave through me. "If she stays too long here, she might not make it."

"C'mon. Drag him up," the sailor said. They pulled out his rotten body three days later. Aron was dead. It was the first fatal diving accident I ever saw. His body was disfigured beyond recognition. Failure to surface on time, the cause of his death only became clear when they flipped over his body. I stood with the commander a few feet away from Aron's lifeless body. Sequential tears on his spine, massive bleeding, and deep wounds had killed this man. Aron died of a shark attack.

That memory made me feel dizzy. I felt numb, and my legs went cold. I was too shocked, maybe because I had never anticipated this. This vessel, the team, the sea was repulsing me. I felt nauseous. I wanted to sleep. I wanted to die because someone was near to death because of my ambitions.

"Hey! Are you feeling alright?" asked David.

"Hmm…I just need a few minutes alone," I said.

"I know we try to avoid reality. Someone dies every day. But today is not our day. Trust me!" he said.

David's words comforted me from the inside. Though I never showed it to him and chose to walk barefoot to the deck. "Listen! We might need to send Sonia back to the shore. She needs emergency care," said David as he changed his latex gloves, and dumped the old ones into the dustbin. I turned back. "What? How?"

"I have called in the chopper. Navy who lent us this vessel… They can send in a helicopter too. Chopper ETA is 6 p.m.," he replied.

I sighed and turned back with a heavy heart. Sonia had to go. We were nowhere close to our objective and already one member less. My eyes got wet. *How could we not see that coming? Poor Sonia. She is in so much pain. God forbid if something happens to her….* I cried myself to sleep for a few hours.

Loud noise and movement on the deck woke me up. I refreshed my blurry eyes. I left the bed and headed to the main deck. There in the corridor, I could see Samira rushing to bring in something. I intuitively understood that Sonia's exfiltration was in process. "Come on here, we need you," said Anish as he glanced at my half-asleep body.

"Where is she?" I asked.

"Chopper's comin' in," he said. I peeped at my watch which reflected 5:45 p.m. I hurried myself up into the open. David sat near the medical stretcher, holding Sonia's hand. I was surprised to see his nurturing side. David looked up right at me and told Sonia of my presence. She was in a pretty bad shape. Her flesh was deeply pierced and her thigh almost dried up from the blood. I kneeled down to her and held her hand. She had a burning fever. "You are going to be okay. We are going to get you out of here," I said. I could see tears rolling on either side of her eyes. The pain of not being able to continue the mission was unsettling for her. Sonia wanted to be a part of this expedition so badly. I felt sad for her and myself.

A few minutes later, Anish and Samira came up on the bridge. And as the sea breeze tried to cover up the dearth of positivity in our heads, the whirring blades cutting through the air became apparent. A shiny object from the west side grew larger and larger. The chopper's engine was powerful enough to mark its presence in the endless sea. It was a Sea King helicopter operated by Navy group for rescue operations. Anish and David shot flairs into the sky, and within moments, the pilots noticed the vessel. The Sea King hovered directly over us. The engine noise and the down thrust were almost impossible to bear. A steel hoist lowered from the helicopter with a metal hook at the end and a metal latch.

Helicopter's doorman radioed in to hook Sonia's stretcher to the hoist. Anish and Samira helped each other out to pull the stretcher. David radioed in for pulling confirmation and Samira waved her hands to the chopper's doorman. There we saw Sonia rise up to around 80 feet into the air, suspended with a steel cable. The crew watched her go with their heads constantly scanning the helicopter. They pulled Sonia's stretcher inside and the aircraft made a rapid U-turn in the air. The noise faded away as the Sea King got smaller. Sonia, our beloved crew member, disappeared with the shiny tiny metal dot in the sky.

Day 13

"Rekindling the courage."

"Friday, the thirteenth… never saw that comin'," Samira made a comment as we all sat for breakfast. "I am already missing Sonia. She made breakfast with all her heart," Anish remarked. The two of them had cultivated a strong bond. Anish seemed genuinely sad after Sonia's departure to the shore. It was a worrisome fact for me.

"How is she now?" I asked David who was busy eating the half-burnt toast he had made and simultaneously working on his laptop.

He looked at me and said, "I wasn't able to set up contact with them. Will retry in a few minutes. Apparently, there had been a storm along the west coast last night as per our radar." I was just not ready to imagine another bad incident. I just hoped that the helicopter landed all fine onto the coast. I kept looking at the SATCOM phone impatiently.

Our plans were hanging thin. Nobody was motivated enough to dive again. The treasure probably sat much below. Though we were too exhausted to think about it, at least for now.

"David! Come along." I invited him for a chat as I left the mission room. David came along and we found ourselves sitting in the storeroom. It smelt like rust in there. The room was full of old stuff, junk; spare parts that probably belonged to the company that leased us the vessel. "What do we do now, David?"

"What do you mean? Do what?" he replied nonchalantly.

"The incident! Sonia is absent. Crew's spirit is broken. We have limited time for the mission. What do we do now?" I asked him.

"Hmmm," he sighed. "Let's give them today. Let them process the trauma. We will begin the dives from tomorrow on."

I agreed with him. "I am worried about Anish," I said.

"Why?" he asked.

"He is too moved by Sonia's accident. If he loses focus, it would be troublesome for all of us." I expressed my concern to him.

"You worry too much, Donna! He'll be fine. Men know how to handle themselves." Somehow, David's words pumped up new light into my eyes. "Let's give them a day. I will be reworking on our mission strategy," said David. "And by the way, I forgot to tell you something very interesting," he said as he suddenly stopped while exiting the storeroom.

"What? Tell me." He had all my attention.

"This morning, I dropped in an underwater drone, remotely operated, to 3000 metres. I got traces of metal all over beneath us."

I felt a sudden rush of blood in my limbs. My sadness faded away for a moment. I got the tunnel vision for a few seconds. "Whaaat!!??" I was awed. I rushed up to David, held him by the neck and kissed him the hardest I could. It was my happiness oozing out through my reflexive kissing.

While I lost myself in the heat of the moment and temporary gratification, Samira walked in on us. Good that she did not see us in that position. David was looking really surprised as if he wasn't sure how to react. Anish just contacted the base. "Sonia's chopper landed safely last evening. She is at the navy hospital. We will get regular updates."

"What does the doctor say?" David asked Samira.

"A surgery would make her fine, but no activity for another month or so." I was too happy with the news David gave me that I almost forgot the intensity of Sonia's situation.

"She'll be back!" David said as he exchanged his gaze briefly with me and Samira while exiting the rusty room.

Day 14

"Just do it!"

I was particularly anxious about the fourteenth morning. We had improvised. I was a witness to failed plans. And I had also seen improvised plans succeed. The past few days had been boring. Yesterday was a tragic one. Sonia's absence was being felt. The doctor said it'll take at least a month for her to recover. David told me about the possibility of our secret mission leaking to the authorities. Since Sonia was on land, she might be interrogated about the incident. Even the media would highlight her rescue. I wanted to consult David. I went to the lower deck and knocked on the door.

"Yes please," he replied from inside. I entered the room. David was shaving in front of the vanity mirror. He looked at me through the mirror before washing his face.

"I was wondering if our mission details would be questioned by the authorities," I said in a worried tone.

"You're worried that Sonia is on the shore. She might spill all the secrets…!" David replied.

I raised my brow, unimpressed by his gesture, and asked, "We need to make sure that Navy keeps the details confidential."

"They will. They want the piece of cake too. I had a word with Sonia on the SAT phone yesterday," David said, looking at me.

"What did you tell her?" I asked, instantly.

"That she is still a part of the team. Simple, Donna. I told her that she will get the piece of cake that we are going to hunt. She took that shark's wrath for the team," David said with a smile. "By the way, Samira apparently spilled the secret of that kiss to Anish. I heard them talking." David said. I didn't flinch a nerve on the outside. I chose not to react.

I began feeling that things were falling out of my hand. Samira could not be trusted. Though we were about to dive together, and the briefing was about to start. I walked up to the pantry and made myself a sandwich. A cup of coffee and a sandwich was what I needed at the moment. 'Now I feel like I did something wrong. There will be consequences. Or maybe I am over thinking.' I kept fighting with my head.

Sudden warning sirens caught my attention. I rushed out to the control room. Seeing nobody, I radioed in, "Crew! What's that siren for?" After a brief static, someone radioed back, "Storm… storm… storm…"

I rushed to the deck. Anish and David stood at each side of the stern as if looking for something.

"Samira! Samira!" Anish shouted at the top of his voice. My instinct immediately alarmed me of an ongoing emergency.

"Samira…. Samira!" shouted David. I rushed towards the men. The deck was wet; waves raging unpredictably. The ocean was restless all of a sudden.

"What happened?" I asked them.

"Samira is missing," Anish said.

"Why are we looking for her 'outside the vessel'?" My heart anticipated the worst.

"She was last seen going to the deck. Anish saw her," said David.

I began calling her name to the ocean. I hurried back inside the vessel, checked all chambers, engine room, radio and navigation room, nothing! My heart started pounding. 'We are not ready for another one of this. God, not again,' I couldn't stop thinking. I went back to the deck. "Anish, when did you see her on the deck?"

"About an hour ago," he said.

"Ask David to anchor." Now, I was determined to take control of the situation. "No other accident is happening under my watch and no one's gettin' hurt."

David suggested a motorboat search and rescue. We planned to trace back the vessel's path. The crew was still not sure where Samira was. We were certain that a wave washed her off the deck.

"Down, down!" David signalled Anish as he lowered the motorboat.

I had a fair experience of riding motorboats in the wild waters. One push of the throttle punched a hundred horses into the sea, and I turned the motorboat into the reverse direction. We cruised back 10 or so miles. David held the binoculars and scanned across. Forty minutes in and no trace of Samira. The water was ice cold. If she had fallen, she would be just minutes away from hypothermia (a medical emergency that occurs when your body loses heat faster than it can produce heat, causing a dangerously low body temperature), and probably her last breath. Waves hit our small metal-ribbed boat and drenched both of us. The clouds were getting denser, light fading away. With every minute, our hopes dwindled like the waves.

"Did you spot her?" Anish radioed in David.

"Not yet. Will keep you updated," David said.

By now, we had searched almost 50 square kilometres of sea. The most probable areas to find Samira were empty. I looked at David. His eyes reflected disappointment and guilt, the guilt of not being able to find her. "We'll find her," I said, without any hope myself. David suggested making a final pass before heading back to the vessel. The waves were getting more furious.

"No success. We are heading back," I radioed in Anish.

As we sped the rescue boat towards the vessel, I kept thinking of the possible place Samira could be. I was not able to accept the bitter reality of not being able to find her. All I wanted to do was to spot her magically somewhere in the waters and save her. David knelt down on one side of the boat, still aimlessly scanning for the trace of anything remotely resembling a human figure.

"There she is, David! David! There..." I pointed towards the vessel's dorsal fin. A yellow inflatable life-vest had caught my eye. It had to be Samira. It was a mandatory safety procedure for the crew to carry the life-vest at all times while on the deck. David hurriedly prepped the ropes to take her in. As I slowed the boat at the rear of the N45, we both made visual contact with the half-dead Samira.

Day 15

"The time has come..."

I had just come back from fishing. It was a long humid day. Hours of patience bore me no fruit. I just wanted to rush to my bed and close my eyes. Maybe tomorrow's sun would bring me some new hope. My home stopped being the home long ago. I found solace only in the laps of the ocean or in the solitude of my own company. I remember a frequently occurring dream that would wake me up in the middle of the nights. Dad drunk, beating up my mom; breaking things, and mom crying... not for herself, but for me. If I could only undo one thing from my life, it would be this dream. Mom crying, me losing, fading away... into the darkness... never to return... forever gone and then suddenly, the brightest of light would hit my forehead.

I woke up gasping for air. Took me a few moments to realize who and where I was. Ahh! Again... the same bad dream. A sudden thought of Samira caused me to hustle up. I put on my shoes, grabbed the radio and went to see her. Anish stood at her door and watched her.

"How is she?" I whispered into his ear, almost perplexing him.

Anish tilted back, "Her fever isn't going down, but she'll recover."

David said, "She is a fighter. Few more minutes in the ice-cold water would have stopped her heart."

As Anish moved to leave me with Samira, he took my hand and kissed it, "Thanks, Donna!" I looked him in the eyes to pacify him and he walked away into the corridor.

I sat close to Samira, held her hand in mine. She was indeed burning with fever. I was, though, at relief. She looked much better than yesterday. David recommended a close care for her. We barred Samira from diving for the next few days until she fully recovered from the extreme temperature exposure. I covered her with the blanket, and left the room. I kept the radio close to her head, in case she needed our help.

A few steps later I found myself joining the boys in the leisure room. The boys had created a light ambience for everyone to relax. David sat on a chair reading the book with a cigar in between his lips. Anish sat on top of a table and was eating a banana. They glanced at me briefly, registering my presence in the room. I casually checked my watch. It was 4:30 p.m. I had slept at 2 a.m. last night. It was a weary night indeed.

"Tomorrow we find whatever has been lying under this vessel. The hunt begins. We are already being challenged by time. It is our turn to punch back," David said, supremely determined, as he walked away, lighting up a cigarette.

A small fire lit deep inside my heart; somewhere my hope had started breathing. I was surprised because I could see myself smiling inside the head, for David. As he walked out of the door, I gazed at him continuously, till he disappeared. David's motivation was strongly driven. He was very casual about the treasure, though he had started displaying the grit and 'I am the man here' attitude. I knew very well. I knew that I was the reason. He had a thing for me. Deep inside his heart, somewhere there was a place for me, the innocent unprotected girl who longed for his affection.

Day 16

"Treasure, treasure, your chest is mine."

Sleeping would have been impossible last night, and so it was. After facing unforeseeable obstacles, almost losing two crew members, and surviving in a 'not so strong' vessel for fifteen days, it was finally the time. I was up before everyone else (it was happening after a long time). It was 4:30 a.m. The submarine was comparatively dark because of the switched-off lights. My spirit was high enough. I was missing Sonia, though! I went in to check on Samira. As I let myself and the light in, I found an empty bed.

"Samira!" As the full view of her room came upon me, I saw her standing weekly close to the bathroom door, standing like a zombie. "Hey!" I rushed to support her. One touch of her hand instantly revealed the fever she was burning in.

"Big day today! I am coming with you, Donna," Samira said, shivering.

"No Samira! We cannot let you in, especially in this condition," I said. "We cannot afford to lose you. You'll be assisting us from the deck. Here, lay down!" I said as I eased her up on the bed. Surprisingly, she was in a half-sleep state and was murmuring in her sleep. I left her sleeping on her bed.

I poured myself a cup of coffee and went into the engine room. The engine room used to be hot. It was chilling in the corridors, so engine room it was. There I sat amidst the deafening noise of the 6,400 horsepower diesel engines running in sync. Noise, coffee, heat, and solitude; the perfect recipe for me to focus. I sat there recalling my best dives and the worst.

My watch beeped at every half-hour interval. It was something that helped me keep a track of time. It was 7 a.m. and I figured the crew was up, as the radio chatter suggested. I went straight to the pantry.

"Ready for the action, Donna?" Anish smiled at me as he made himself a toast.

"Indeed!" I said. I went to David to know more about what we were looking for. He stood in the mission room with his arms folded, blue t-shirt and cargo pants made him look fitter than he actually was. He was glaring at the map on the wall. He smiled at me.

"So, what are we looking for today? I know it is not the Nizam's treasure, still…" I asked.

"Something heavy. Metal. Precious one. My Sonar caught it right below where we are," he replied.

My heart was thrilled. The team had to learn to coordinate. "So, what's the plan?" I asked.

"Well! We grab the equipment," he said while pointing towards a particular place on the map, "deploy ourselves here…

and… reach…" Before he could finish, my lips locked with his. I caught him by surprise and he fell for it. Both of us had got fired-up, the passion was rekindled, and suddenly the world seemed conquerable. Before we could go any further, he got conscious and both of us pulled back.

I have seen my Mom and Dad surviving a loveless marriage. Mom was the legit sufferer; dad used alcohol to numb his frustration, which only backfired at his perception of reality. I wish my parents could show me what love looked like. Every girl believes in fairy tales, that a knight will someday take away her heart. Abuses and curses, that is all my mind had registered, and that is all it had learned.

David was my knight. I could see it in his eyes. His face lit up, and he locked his eyes with mine. "Let's get the treasure, Donna," he said.

"Of course," I replied as he set my hair fringe behind my ear. That melted my heart. "Ask everyone to assemble at the deck with the equipment; I'll be there to brief them!" David said before he left the room after kissing my forehead. Somehow, I was convinced that I had found something worthwhile and fulfilling.

At the deck, David stood at the side. I and Anish faced him from the side of the vessel. The equipment lay in between us. Samira came up on the deck to join us. "Alright, crew," said David, "The hunt is on. This is going to be our 'actual' first diving mission. We are looking for a chest or… a box maybe, with unknown content inside. It should be within a radius of 400 metres with the submarine as the center point." The crew listened attentively while Samira tried her best to keep up with him.

"So, the plan is this. Donna, Anish and I will go down through the anchor rope. We will use the rope as the reference point. Then we will trace 400 metres in different directions until we sweep the whole area for that chest. Samira will keep up the communication system going and will stand-by for any emergency, and will monitor the communication and guide us if we are stuck from the control room." David's plan was straightforward. "We go in. Find what we want. We come back up. We celebrate." David boosted up our spirits. The crew cheered together.

Within fifteen minutes, we all were suited up, standard equipment checked, standard diving checked, and 500 metres of depth. The three of us immersed ourselves into the water slowly, grabbing the anchor rope. David lowered himself gradually. "Watch out for any creature with 'pointy' fins." David laughed over the intercom radio. Bubbles went up as we utilized our oxygen tanks. I found myself again in the hauntingly beautiful depths of the Sentinel waters.

Within the next fifteen minutes, we had lowered ourselves by 400 metres. Anish was some 20 feet above me, clinging on to the rope; David was at around the same distance. The sudden slow rising of the sand from the floor told me that David had touched the sea-floor. I could feel the whistle in my ears and numbness in the skin due to static pressure. "We are there, touched the sea-floor," I radioed Samira.

"Bravo!!" Samira cheered us over the radio.

Anish was gliding over the aquatic floor in the skydiving position. David signaled us to split up and begin exploration.

With thumbs-up affirmation, we parted ways, 400 metres in three different directions. Never in my life had I seen such a variety of life for Ms My shoulder light scanned the floor and the fishes moving in trails. It was the deep sea. Sunlight is forbidden to reach here. Though faintly scattered rays saved us from being in the absolute dark.

I kept swimming, scanning every coral, stone, natural artefact and the life forms that I could. My eyes were searching for a chest, a box. Occasional radio chatter would distract me, but I got used to it. At one point though, my connection was lost and I panicked. Swimming swiftly at such depths was impossible. I had covered just 100 metres straight in the past twelve minutes. 'It must be above the ocean floor,' I thought. 'Probably covered in sand or corals.'

"Found anything?" Anish asked impatiently over the radio. Suddenly, I came across a shiny, broken handle. My flashlight's narrow beam just focused on that man-made sunken object. It was when I moved the beam ahead that I saw a big chest.

"I think I got it," I excitedly informed David.

"What? How does it look like?" he asked.

I moved closer to the chest to get a better picture. The chest was about 3x3x3 feet. "Maroon walls, golden boundaries, wrapped in a chain…" I replied to him.

"That's it! Your location please, Donna," David hurried with Anish towards my location. Within ten minutes, the diver-duo arrived at my location. I updated Samira about our finding. This was our achievement after a fair share of failures. I was glad that I was on this mission.

Now the chest had to be pulled up to the vessel. David and Anish hooked the chained-chest with some kind of anchor. "Let's move. The chest has been hooked. We will tow it with the vessel's hoist."

As we swam up, the water had magically become sparkling. I followed David as he swam like an angel. Anish carried the hook-head to be attached to the hoist. None of us could actually wait to check out what our victory held for us.

A question then hit my mind. "But, how did you know the box by its description, David?"

"I do my homework, darling," he said. "Let's talk when we surface," he said as he went up paddling his fins. Our first mission was successful. "Celebration?"

"Absolutely," Samira announced over the radio.

Day 17

"What have we got?"

It was not a surprise that everyone was on the deck before the sun rose. That was the power of treasures. The beastly metal box had been covered up with tarpaulin. "I am so excited," Samira clenched my arm in excitement. She got a little embarrassed but a sunshine smile enveloped her face again. Anish came up with a heavy dagger. The tool looked crafted in the devil's foundry, such was it appeal.

"Let the spotter open it," David raised his hand and Anish handed him the dagger.

"I wish it holds tons of gold!" Anish was super excited. I wondered how he had even slept last night.

"And now, the time has come," David announced, looking into my eyes.

"Stop being cinematic, break the chain, fast!" I snapped. At one strike, one chain crack open, and with the next four strikes of heavy steel blade, the chest was finally free after years of captivity.

We all gathered around the big box. It was quite an amazing moment. Imagine a group of children finding a puppy in the park. How do they surround it? It was no different with us, except for the puppy we were looking at, quintals of unknown stuff we had just recovered from the dark depths.

Anish and David finally lifted the heavy lid covering the box. A few pushes and the lid detached itself from the box. What we found in there almost skipped our heart beats.

I could not describe the glare it reflected. It held the power of a thousand suns. The golden ruby embedded jewels, wrapped around ancient weapons, swords with hilts crafted from pure gold, and a few scrolls garnished over the riches we had just uncovered. Everyone, including David, had frozen for those few seconds, struck in awe. Nizam's treasure took away those few minutes we could never account for. The beauty surmounting the chest was indescribable.

"O… Holy… Jesus… Christ, what have we done?" Anish lost his sanity for a while. I looked at David, who himself came back to senses minutes later.

"Hey! David. What's up? What's the deal? How did you know about this chest?" I had so many questions for him.

"All I can tell is that the chest is almost valued at around ten million U.S. dollars," David replied.

Samira knelt down, "Ten million… U.S. dollars?"

"Yes," David replied.

"We just became millionaires, just like that," Anish held his head as he roamed back and forth on the deck.

"Let us preserve what we have, and get to the mission deck," David said. The crew walked into the room, still in shock.

We had preserved each and every artifact and object from the chest neatly wrapped into silk-wraps under each other's observation. It was high time. And, without saying, it was party time too.

What followed that night changed my life. We had wine, music and dance. I came closer to David. We had longed for each other for so long. I never wanted the night to end. When my head hit the pillow, I felt proud of ourselves for all that we had accomplished, as each day counted and each day we were doing something great that we truly enjoy. I was feeling more confident, accomplished and noticed an increase in self-esteem. Before I fell asleep, I was smiling to myself because I couldn't wait to start the next day.

Day 18

"Wish and the universe shall conspire to fulfill it."

My eyes snapped open by a thrilling dream. 'Where…? Where am I?' A positive wave of recent memories put a smile on my face as I got off the bed, remembering the treasure.

Everyone was sleeping. It was one of those rare mornings when the vessel's corridors were silent, and on the deck prevailed a sense of peace. I was the first one to wake up in the anchored submarine. The team had nothing planned for the day. To be honest, the number 'ten million' kept circling in my mind. Coffee was all I needed. I grabbed a hot brew from the pantry; I went to the cargo bay, just a level below me. As I entered, a weird sense of dread gripped me. 'Strange!' I thought. Stranger because it was the chamber where our 'riches' were preserved. I walked into the chamber, slowly gliding by the shelves with my coffee. No wonder such wealth can easily mesmerize the mind. 'Treasures do have the power to wage wars and take lives. Isn't that what makes them worth chasing?' I thought.

My eyes caught the view of a scroll. It was gold plated, and writings were engraved on a thin silver base. I kept the coffee mug on an empty shelf and grabbed the scroll. It read –

If you walk upon the earth with a noble heart and kindness, this treasure might be useless to you. But you wage wars over the water to scavenge on the loots of others, this treasure shall be your end.

'Huh! So this was a looted treasure. Oh! And David never told us the story behind it too. I must ask him today.' I wasn't very moved by what was written on the scroll. However, I had enough questions piled up in my head for David. I walked away swiftly from the room, almost forgetting my coffee mug.

I wanted to see David. It was not that early in the morning too. I went to my deck, put on my wristwatch and went to wake the sleepy head up. He wasn't there. My heart almost pounded out of my chest when David shock-surprised me as I turned back. "Stupid you! God… I almost died," I laughed along with him as my shock turned into momentary anger and then melted away with laughter. Regular old David. "How did you sleep last night, sleepy head?" I teased him.

"Very well," he said and we had a good laugh again.

By 10 a.m., everybody was up. Each member did visit the treasure chamber and satisfied their urges to watch massive wealth. 'Let us find the one we are looking for, and let me be there to capture all your reactions to it,' I thought.

It was kind of a day-off for the crew. We planned to navigate slowly ahead while catching some fresh fish and barbequing it. Probably from tomorrow on, the crew would be back to the main mission and expedition would resume. But again, my questions had remained unanswered.

In the afternoon, I caught David off-guard on the deck. He was enjoying the scenic view, lost somewhere in his mental man cave.

"How did you know about this treasure, David?" I asked him straightaway as I took position beside him on the deck rail. "Our equipment is not that capable, and both of us know that," I said.

"We have to pay our dues, Donna," David replied looking at the ocean's far away horizon. "The mission's cost is way beyond the team's imagination."

"What do you mean?" I asked.

"You think a random company will lease a submarine and all the equipment to an amateur team who pitched them a treasure hunt? Huh! We have to pay Fort Bridge somehow," David reasoned, still thinking about something else. "Our expedition's cost is somewhere close to eight million U.S. dollars. The treasure is worth more than that. Hence, it cannot be distributed. The riches we have just acquired have to be paid as our dues."

The picture was getting clearer to me now. "We will tell the crew in the evening." He advised. This treasure was our ticket to the rest of the mission.

"But how did you know it was here?" I asked.

"I got a tip from a Navy inside official. He has a cut in this. He had narrowed down the area for me. This treasure was actually being searched by a diving party a few months ago. They met their fate in the sea, however. That mission was sponsored by Fort Bridge as well."

I appreciated his steps and planning to fuel the mission. This was a genuine man. Though, what I had suspected eventually regarding the treasure, came true a few days later.

Day 19

"Satisfaction is the enemy of success, have it not until you make it."

Everyone surrounded the table at 7 a.m. sharp. Maps, compasses, and a few notes lay cluttered over it. "We are running at full power, surfaced. Should hit the Dive Point Bravo in an hour," Anish announced over the radio.

"Just an hour to the target. For the mission we've waited for so long." David started briefing the team. "Kola Regio" was our call sign for the supposed area where Nizam's treasure was located. The point was only a few miles from the main Sentinel island, and a few miles from our then current location. "Anish and Donna, this is going to be a tough one. We got the previous one easily; should not soar your hopes high. Though, if found, we'll be changing ours and many other lives forever. This is a massive treasure. Keep your eyes open at all times. Clear?" David asked. Everyone nodded in affirmation, with enthusiasm. "Rendezvous at the deck in two," he instructed.

We all hustled up to the deck, one by one. The vessel was moving pretty fast; never realized it when we were inside it. The way the submarine was cutting through the waters pumped me with thrill. The idea that thousands of horsepower was challenging the sea and succeeding was just fascinating. The three of us gathered on the slightly swinging open deck, while Samira navigated the vessel from the navigation chamber.

"Anish and Donna, come up to me," said David. We did so. "Donna! Stand behind Anish. Anish, fold your hands and fall freely backwards. You, Donna will keep him from falling down," he said. We were all perplexed by the nature of the exercise.

"Are you sure?" I asked.

"You'll see girl, just do it," David pushed. The waves smashed against the railing just then, drenching everyone with the fresh sea water. The crew smelt like salt. As soon as Anish fell freely backwards, I caught him. I had strong arms, which was a surprise to me. David clapped. "Anish and Donna, now swap your positions. Anish will now catch you," said David. Again, the same exercise was repeated with Anish catching the strong lady. "Bravo!" cheered David. The same exercise was repeated twice with the combination of pairs on the deck.

We were all ready for him to explain why we did what we just did. I fired the question at him. "The point here is to breed trust between the team members. When we fall, and someone catches us, our subconscious mind begins trusting the other person. It is recommended for strong bonding, a common exercise by British and Indian Special Forces operators." I was amazed by David's thought process. 'He never fails to surprise!' I thought. The crew smiled at each other, trying to evade the oncoming wave and not get swept away. "Just a few minutes to Point Bravo, divers. Gather your equipment and assemble here in five," said the man I was falling in love with.

It was 8.15 a.m., and I could imagine the trail of hydro-turbulence our vessel had created to propel us to this point. N45 came to a halt, anchored. Samira joined us on the deck to tally the final strategy. Anish had prepared the diving plan, being an expert in the field. "Donna and I will cover the western flank of the Kola Regio spot. David will cover the southern flank. Each of us will carry forty minutes of oxygen. The target depth is 150 metres." We were all ears to his plan. "From there on, we will begin the search for our target," Anish said as he equipped himself with the oxygen cylinder.

"Samira will monitor the communication channels, water parametres, and any change in the surrounding that can affect our mission," David wound up the briefing.

Within five minutes, I found myself and the others heavily loaded with the gear. It was time. The moment I had waited for so long stood right in front of me. It was my turn to take action.

"Ready for the action, babe?" Samira smiled at me.

"Always," I said, putting on my mask.

Anish, David and I gave thumbs up to each other. Samira took her place in the control room. We threw ourselves into the ice-cold water one by one; same old feeling. The sensation of infinity, thrill and fulfillment wrapped me from head to toe. This was beyond contemplation for those who live and die in mediocrity.

Anish was beneath me, gradually lowering himself towards the ocean floor. David parted ways with us at some 30 metres. His faintly visible shoulder lights became invisible after a while. At such depths, divers should always be careful of bends. Lowering oneself too fast can cause excruciating pain, even death. I could only see Anish's lights focusing in various directions once in a while just beneath me. The water at this point was too salty, as reflected by a very few numbers of small fishes.

"Heading to the southern flank," David said over the radio.

"At the sea-floor," Anish said. Soon, I too touched the bottom of the ocean and announced over the radio and then began the search of our lifetimes.

The floor was muddy. Occasional appearance of octopus and other exotic life forms did dazzle me. Anish signalled me to check out a raised structure, probably a drowned medium-sized boat. I went up to it only to confirm my guess. "I am at the drowned wooden boat. It says *Midwest 1934* on its stern side," I radioed in the team.

"Leave no stone unturned," David replied.

"Be assured," I replied back to him.

Ten minutes passed by… Then twenty… We had only a few minutes of oxygen left with us. Surfacing was the only option. "This is shooting arrows in the blind. The area is too wide to search for the signs of the treasure. We need to iterate our strategy. See you all at the surface," David declared.

"True that, we need specific spots. We have limited oxygen supply too. Let's call it a day," I declared as well.

Within the next six minutes, the crew once again floated above the water. It was a broad search strategy. We needed a better one. I made up my mind to formulate a plan myself. We unloaded the equipment and put on dry clothes. "Yo guys! I will need loads of coffee and notes for a new exploration plan. Bear with me in the night," I said.

Everyone worked silently in their chambers that night. Maps and notes could be found on the beds. Brainstorming was on. We were just getting started.

Day 20

"Be a good reader. Especially when it comes to people's intentions."

My wristwatch selflessly beeps at the best hours of the day. It was 8 in the morning and we had a lot of academic work to do that day. I dressed and left the room. My body ached a little from all the hard work I had done 150 metres down. A mild, sweet honey aroma caught my attention. My senses detected the approaching subject of happiness. *Pancakes, yayy*! My senses just couldn't resist the temptation and I landed straight into the pantry. "Wow! Samira, never knew you were so good at… cooking!" I said.

"Grab some, before they eat it all, here, take the maple syrup," she said as she served me the yummiest fluffy pancakes ever.

"Thanks, babe, you made my day," I expressed my heartfelt gratitude to her as I exited the pantry.

I remember how my mom made pancakes every summer. I used to come back from the school, and before I could go swimming with my friends, I had to eat her delicious pancakes, special ones full of love.

David was immersed in his book. "Hey! Where is Anish?" I asked them.

"Don't know, might be downstairs. Why?"

"Nothing," I said as I went to the engine room and the navigation room. No signs of him! 'Maybe he is in the loo' the thought crossed my mind. As I began ascending the stairs, a clunking noise caught my attention. The sound came from the lower level, from the cargo bay where the gala treasure was kept. My mind got filled with a cloud of doubtful thoughts.

I walked down with silent toes, being as stealthy as possible. What I saw when I peeped surprised me to the core. I saw a human figure lurking behind the shelves. Its slight movement revealed that it was Anish. He was sneaking up on the treasure. Whether he was stealing or not, I did not know for sure. He was probably about to go for a valuable piece, I guess. It was then when I made a stupid mistake. I stepped over a loose metal panel, making a noticeable sound: Anish no doubt noticed it. By now, he knew that he was being spied. I immediately ran up the stairs. I had to be fast so that he never knew it was me who had caught him 'in the act.' He knew that somebody saw him stealing. But who it was, he never knew.

My daylight was spent in calculating Anish as a person. What I saw was certainly true. The question was, did he do it out of greed? Or was he present amongst us for a more damaging reason? I wasn't sure what to do. One thing to remember is that everyone has different moral codes and ideas about how life should be lived, and we don't find out these differences until something happens. But this is how we see people's true colours; we get to see who they really are not the same person we thought they were. Nevertheless, I decided to keep the secret with myself and continue to keep a tab on his activities and intentions.

"You cannot get hurt by people, Donna," my mom said to me in a concerned manner, as if teaching me a life lesson. I was terrible when it came to judging people. "Easily trusting people leaves you vulnerable. You must stay sharp, my darling." Since then, trust and integrity are what makes for my league of people.

That night, we all sat across together for dinner after a tiresome day. Anish sat right beside me. He smiled while chewing the food and went back to focus on his meal. I ate and was numb to the talking and laughter that went on the table. My eyes would somehow return back to Anish. Occasional smiles between me and him removed me from his suspect radar. Though I noticed how he would fix his cold dead stare at Samira.

"I am done guys. I am off to bed. Long day tomorrow. Good night." I wished the team as I exited the scene.

Day 21

"Life is a thousand battles.
Be a victor in each of them."

It was like any other morning aboard the surfaced submarine. Except that the air was a little confused; we had slightly tasted success recently. I sat alone in the pantry with my coffee. My head echoed negative anticipation. It screamed of sinister events that were yet to manifest. The most challenging of all resistance comes from within. The similarity with all warriors is that they're always battling demons within themselves. It's a constant battle that has to be fought non-stop.

The corridor speakers suddenly blasted with, "Donna! Donna, we need you in the mission room." It was David.

"I'll be right there," I radioed him. I rushed to the mission room. "Hey, what's up?" I asked Anish and David.

"We have devised a new strategy to search the treasure. We reckon that it is much closer to the main Sentinel island," Anish explained.

"Well, how close?" I asked the obvious question.

"Much much closer, Donna. Approximately a mile or two from the island," David said while calibrating the GPS.

"Well that sounds good; I mean we can camp on the island…" I suggested.

"Hmm…" David affirmed.

"Everyone!" Samira came running to the room.

"What is it?" asked Anish.

"We received information on our radio just now," she said. "We have a chopper inbound, ETA five minutes." The three of us rushed to the open deck. Why would there be a chopper? We had no information about any aircraft.

"Do you know what this is about?" I asked David.

The pilot radioed. "We have three minutes to drop the package, be ready."

"Package?" asked Anish. We were all perplexed.

"Did we ask for any supplementary aids?" Samira asked all of us. Nobody knew the answer. We just knew that the chopper belonged to Navy Corp.

The chopper soon appeared over our vessel, hovering perpendicular to the deck. It stayed perfectly still at about 50 feet in the air. David signalled with his hands about chopper's relative position to the vessel's service. A hoist with a mesh carried box soon lowered towards the deck. It came down swinging amidst the turbulent air and engine noise from the helicopter. By that time, we were all keen enough to pounce at the large carry-box. As soon as the box touched the deck, my morning blues turned into a happy, cheerful memory. Sonia was back! And, with her, my strength grew a hundred folds. It was hard to describe how the crew felt at her arrival. David, Anish, and Samira were genuinely glad to have Sonia back. I became stronger in an instant, with her powerful presence.

That night, we celebrated Sonia's comeback, and I had a lot to talk to her about. We also showed her our recently unearthed riches. Sonia was overwhelmed with her welcome. I was looking forward to using her skills in the main mission that was to start from the next day. Pieces of destiny were falling into place as I noticed that life begins to feel pretty effortless. Great things make appearances at the right time and place often, and the good really begins to outweigh any of the bad. Things were looking up overall, and I knew more good things were on my way.

Day 22

"Stop. Adapt. Acclimatize. Charge."

Sonia bought freshness with her, something that had been missing on the vessel for the last couple of days. Even though we had found the treasure, it reminded us of our capabilities. Our victory was not complete. It was finally the time to undertake the mission we were all here for. All of us gathered on the deck that morning.

We were supposed to discuss our findings and notes that we had prepared a day before. It was time to analyze the insights on the treasure hunt by each member, and explain everything to Sonia. "Alright... The agenda for this meeting is to discuss a starting point for the treasure hunt. We need to narrow down our exploration parametre," I said as the cool sea breeze blew my hair over the face. "Who's starting?" I asked the crew. Samira raised her hand. "Please," I indicated her to take my position and speak freely. She opened up a brown leather pad and began reciting her notes.

"I analyzed all the previous missions carried out to find the Nizam's treasure. The supposed area is actually not far away from here, only 20-30 miles west of this point. We might be looking for our target close to the North Sentinel island. In the previous expeditions, divers covered up at least 7 square miles of the deep sea with the average depth of 250 metres," she concluded.

"Okay, and what kind of artifacts or objects are we actually looking for?" Anish posed an intelligent question.

David stood up and said, "There is no reliable description of the treasure. We do, however, have some unofficial accounts of the divers who claim to have been close to the treasure. Only if they weren't hallucinating, haha!" David cracked a joke which was not funny. Nobody laughed. At extreme depths, hallucinations do occur. It is caused by the inhalation of nitrogen gas at high pressure, a state similar to drunkennes. Though we did not have anything else other than the unofficial descriptions.

David carried on, "An account from a veteran treasure hunter and diver, Mr Anthony Bergs, says that 'the treasure is too great for any one person. It sits in the heart of the ocean's darkest region, where no man with impure intent can enter. The massive wealth sits inside the huge chests, in the antique statues, in the form of jewels and precious stones. The Royal Fortune treasure is located somewhere inside a complex system of caverns, the mouth of which opens up into the Kola Regio. Of course, I could have become a king with such wealth that I found. But to recover it from its native place is next to impossible. Especially when your crew is dead, and the island in which you were camping is inhabited by man-eaters.' Mr Bergs wrote this piece in 1872 in his diary which was recovered five years after his death."

"The island must be the Sentinel group," Sonia said.

"He said a 'system of caverns'!" Anish exclaimed.

"Man-eaters?" Samira seemed scared.

"The crew was dead?" David had other concerns, obviously.

"Nobody said the treasure would unearth itself and walk up to each of you," I answered all the exclamations with sarcasm.

"Donna, worked on the strategy?" David asked me.

"Yes. Anish and I have worked out a strategy for diving and covering the maximum sea-floor with minimum oxygen."

Anish got up and explained, "No two divers will cover the same area twice. With a single cylinder, or maximum two, each diver will be responsible to explore the assigned sections. This will boost our search efficiency."

"On the top of that, we will undergo an acclimatization course that we have designed to warm up your bodies and minds for extreme conditions. We will start with them right away. Our first dive section setting and dive will be tomorrow. In an hour, we all shall begin with our course for the real world. Once the acclimatization is complete, we will position the N45 in the area suggested by Samira," I said while concluding the meeting.

About an hour later, all of us gathered over the cold submarine deck. All of our equipment lay in front of us. I was back in my instructor mode. It was time to toughen up the crew for success.

The first task for the divers was to put on their life jacket, dive into the water, swim freestyle to a marked yellow floating buoy at 50 metres, and then return to the vessel. I had learnt this technique from a Japanese diving instructor. He said it toughened the mind against shock, boost confidence and built endurance required for deep sea dives. I was just following his words of wisdom. "Divers, ready! Set pose… hooyah! Take deep breaths…1… 2… 3… 1… 2… 3…" I burst out with energy. "You have 100 metres to cover back and forth in this ice-cold water." All of them listened. "On Anish's mark, you'll dive at once. The winner gets this antique ring we found in the treasure. On your marks, go!"

As I waved the divers off to the sprint towards the buoy, I myself dove to ensure fairness on their part. Samira was super fast in the beginning, though she lost pace at the mid-point. David did manage a mediocre pace consistently. In the end, however, Sonia was the one to touch the yellow floating buoy first. She immediately turned her buxom body backward and swam back to the N45 at a medium speed, only to claim the antique ring. The crew seemed exhausted after the priming round. "C'mon, you've just warmed up. Time for pushups… Here is the deal. Twenty pushups in each set, 40-second interval between each set." I began myself as I spoke. They couldn't resist. Within seconds, the bodies got heated up. The crew was coming in form.

"Anish, your crew now!" I handed the crew lead to him.

"This is the divers watch. Turn by turn you'll put it on," he said. "The target is to dive as deep as possible with just the goggles and the snorkel. The watch will record the maximum depth you reach. Then surface and the next diver will go." Anish instructed.

David could do 8 metres. His high bone-density demanded bigger lungs and breathe holding capacity for diving without cylinder.

"Next," Anish called. Samira touched 12 metres mark, diving straight like a hunting arrow. Sonia could do five, and I did ten myself. Anish then gave us tips for better posture and we listened.

It was crucial to spool up the crew, both physically and mentally, before the actual hunt began. We all practiced and improvised, assisted each other, and competed against ourselves. We burnt away our laziness until we all were exhausted. That night, we all ate too much because of the training we had done. Tomorrow was going to be a remarkable day.

Day 23

"Your dreams will manifest once you decide to take control."

Crew positioned the vessel close to the Sentinel island, the night before. Main island's shore was visible from the deck. It was some 2-3 miles from our location. Anish and David were busy mapping the spots for setting up the buoy sections. We all agreed to go two divers at a given point of time. This way we minimized the risk and maximized the crew support for each diving member with limited oxygen.

Finally, David and Anish came up with thirty 'diving hotspots' to begin our treasure hunt with. Sonia worked out all the equipment while Samira gave submarine's hoist and auxiliary power systems another round of checks. We all agreed to one more important point. No diver was supposed to be in the water after 6 p.m. "The weather does not look happy today," Samira came up on the deck to me.

"How bad do you think?" I asked.

The winds were mild; the climate was cool. It was the typical indicator of an approaching thunderstorm. "Thunderstorm… that might last overnight," Samira said.

"Okay, then let us carry out our first dive before the conditions get worse," I pushed her to notify others.

8:00 a.m.

"The buoys have been planted. Sonia and I have marked seven of them. Each diver shall be able to dive down with the reference rope anchored from the buoy and explore an area of 300 square metres in a single go," I explained. "Though, ask David and Anish regarding the rope's radius," I said. I stood up, tied my hair and took out my wallet. An old picture of my beautiful mother froze me in time.

"Worst of conditions always begin to surmount once you decide to take your first step. It comes with many faces. Fear of even starting, failing, negative anticipation and what not," she said as I wiped away my tears. "But why has Dad asked me to drop this year at college? I need to study, mom," I remember those exact words. "I know, beautiful. Time is the greatest master of all. It is the only source of wisdom, existence and eternal knowledge known to man. Trust it. Time is a tough examiner. Though it gives you chances. The only thing it demands in return is unlimited courage to never give up," Mom said as she lay ill on the bed. "Fear no failure, fear not death. Even success can bring fear of losing what you just gained. Contemplate your existence, and you shall see the bigger picture yourself."

Bigger picture! Those words always get to me. I folded the wallet and put it inside the bag. It was time to unwrap my favourite scuba mask, and best gear (something I had been waiting to open up on this very day). I felt like a little child who just could not help but play with the new toys. I then went up to the deck for breakfast. It was planned that the first two divers will start at 9:30 a.m.

Anish and Samira were going in first. Samira was supposed to cover the western flank, and Anish covered the right flank. They carried oxygen worth thirty minutes and high luminescence flashlights with them. Depth was around 220 metres, and the visibility underwater was fair enough. "Check!"

"Check, coming in Samira," both the divers checked their communication equipment.

Within minutes, I found myself in the control room with David and Sonia and the divers began descending down to the sea-floor.

9:45 a.m.

Whenever Anish or Samira radioed in, I could hear the distinct disturbance of underwater turbulence caused by the divers' bodies and occasional air bubbles. "Eight minutes to sea floor," Anish declared.

"What about you Samira?" David asked over the wireless intercom.

"Ten minutes," she replied. Both the divers were to be monitored separately due to different diving sections.

9:55 a.m.

Both the divers landed on the sea floor just minutes before. Both of them communicated simultaneously over the radio. Both the divers glided close to the sea floor. We kept navigating them and David simultaneously marked the explored areas on the map. Sonia kept an eye on their vital signs and oxygen levels. It was a silent mission for the next few minutes.

10:20 a.m.

"My radius is covered. I got nothing here. No trace of any artefact," Anish said.

"What about you, Samira?" I asked. No response. "Samira, what is your status?" I repeated over the radio.

"Surf… surf…" her broken voice echoed through our earpieces. She seemed in distress.

"Samira! Samira!" we shouted over the radio microphones.

"Alert Donna, we have a possible emergency," David said in haste to me. I just grabbed my snorkel and scuba mask to prepare for any rescue activity.

"Keep me updated," I radio checked in with Sonia and David as I exited the control room.

I hurried to the deck, stood their scanning the water. It was calm and quiet. All the more disturbing, since she had not surfaced yet. "What is the update?" I asked the control room crew over the radio.

"Her radio is silent. She must surface in a minute or two," said Sonia.

"I am going in on her diving section," I said as I had already stepped into the water. I could see the orange buoy meant to guide her in the western flank. I took a deep dive. It must have hardly been 3 or 4 metres. I saw a fast-moving body emerge just beneath me. Before I could take any action, the body surfaced. It was Samira. I was so glad to see her. But she was still in distress.

"Move! Move, gam of sharks is all around," she said with a shiver. I was surprised because I could not see fins. I peeked inside the water and looked at a distance. The closest shark, to my bone chilling view, was just a few feet away from us.

Samira and I swam with all our might. We eventually disturbed more water as our legs fluttered, attracting more of them. I remember while swimming to the vessel, I turned back once. There were at least five fins racing towards us. There was no time to radio in, call for help, or possibly do anything rational at that point. Almost 30 metres of explosive freestyle swimming bought both of us back to the safety of the vessel. I remember Samira lying down immediately on the floor and passing out. I sat down, all exhausted. David and Sonia soon rushed to our aid.

"Anish is still out there," I said. "Tell him to keep an eye on his surrounding, and not disturb too much of water." David instructed Anish. For safety, the motorboat was deployed cruising in it, bringing Anish aboard in one piece.

"They are probably here for the mating season," Sonia's insight helped a little. "Sharks must vacate this area within twelve hours and move on to a new spot." We all looked down from the deck, numerous bladed fins passing by.

The day became too much of an adventure as the crew was unaware of the finned killing machines surrounding the vessel.

Day 24

"Something is better than nothing…"

My mom used to tell me, "You have brains in your head. You have feet in your shoes. You can steer yourself in any direction you choose. You're on your own. And you know what you know. And YOU are the one who'll decide where to go." I often said to her, "Wow! That is beautiful, mommy." Those words echoed in my dreams I guess my mom was my spirit guide. My ambitions were made out of her soul, her pain, her smiles, and her faith. *"You are destined to win, dear," she had always told me.*

I woke up to the beeps of my wrist watch. It was 7:30 a.m. I realized I just had a dream. Last day's events were a little unsettling for me. I could see those shark fins approaching me. I do not have any inherent fear of sharks or carnivores in general. The event was just symbolic of my thoughts and memories that sometimes haunt me to the core. Anyhow, I got up; brushed my teeth. The mirror said I was going to be fine today. I regained my injured willpower, and went to the mission room. Sonia and

David were listening to Indian coast guard's weather forecast over the radio.

"What does the weather say?" I asked them.

"There is a cyclone building up 300 miles south of here. It is headed for the opposite direction, we shall see calm waters here," Sonia broke the news.

"Sounds good. Me and David are going down today. Hey David! Make sure you take the harpoon!" I said grabbing an apple from the table.

8:00 a.m.

Same old routine. Equipment check, radio check, deep breaths and I was good to go. David covered the western section three, I was supposed to explore eastern section four. As I jumped down, a strange feeling engulfed me.

"You are just like your mother. Die. Go to hell," my father yelled at me, drunk as always. "You should have been killed at birth," hurling abuses at me and my mother without remorse. "Hey, shut up! Don't talk to my child like that," mom said wiping away her own tears. Their fights, the loud noise, her pain, his abuse, the chaos, the madness, it was never ending. I wanted to run away far into an island, forever. Mom's tears always held me back. It was later in life that I figured out I was designed to achieve. As mom used to say, "You are a born survivor, Donna. You are designed to achieve and dominate the negativity."

I checked my pressure gauge and the shoulder light. Born to achieve. I am the one. Mom is always right. I am born to achieve, I affirmed myself. The exploration began. I swam close to the ground. The water was shiny blue, and the sand crystals were clearly visible.

8:45 a.m.

Me and David covered acres and acres of sea floor. Some sunken boats caught my eye. Forgotten for years, they loudly screamed of their voyages and stories. I even came across some chests, only to find them empty. I surfaced back with bare hands at 8:55 a.m.

10:00 a.m.

Anish and Sonia went for the second round of exploration in section five and six. They explored the western and eastern flanks, only to return empty handed. Sonia, however, located a statue-like structure far off from her dive section. The crew decided to explore it in the next round of diving.

By afternoon, the divers were exhausted and it was time to organize the data, and some tea.

Radio broadcast echoed of the massive cyclone that hit the southern side just a few hours earlier. As an after effect, thunderstorm clouds started brewing in the sky. Rain fell, forcing us to leave the deck. It was around 7 in the evening. As I exited, I thought I saw a light flash twice, far off in the horizon. Maybe it was just a fig of my tired mind's imagination.

Rest and relaxation were what the crew sought after a sumptuous meal prepared by Anish and Sonia. Tomorrow would be another big day.

Day 25

"Enemies are always close by.
Stay sharp... always."

It was a surprising morning. A wave of confusion and anticipation took the crew by surprise. We all assembled at the deck. For the situation that we were witnessing, we had no playbook. We were just a bunch of explorers with basic diving equipment; operating out of the legal bounds, covertly, far away from the nearest sign of human civilization. The sight was strange in itself. But before that, let me tell you how the morning started.

I was so thankful for Sonia's morning pancakes. "I missed them as bad as you, darling!" I said.

"See, I am back because I couldn't resist the temptation to lure you with them." She replied with her cute signature smile. Sonia, Anish and I sat in the mission room with the breakfast while David and Samira were still sleeping. It was 9:00 a.m.

"Anish, can you get me the diving schedule for today? We might need to hurry," I said. "Losing daylight wouldn't be wise.

Broadcast this over the intercom, and wake those sleepy heads up," I said as I got up with my plate and headed towards the pantry.

As I exited the pantry, I remembered to take a few notes from yesterday. They were recorded in a small memo kept in my room. The moment I was about to enter in there, my radio crackled in, "Crew, this is Anish. I need binoculars on the deck, urgent." His coarse voice echoed all over again, "Binos on upper deck, now, urgent." I was a little worried by now. "Alright, I am coming in," I replied over the radio set.

I took the 60x celestron binoculars up to the deck. Meanwhile, others had already reached the upper deck. It was not until a few minutes later that I gauged the gravity of the whole situation. What we all saw was a small object, far-off on the horizon. It appeared stationary at first. "Zoom in; try to identify what the hell is that?" Samira said with a glimpse of worry on her face. I directed my binos to the point.

"It is a ship. Seems like a wooden one," I said. "Around thirty miles from here."

"Can you see the naval identity number on it?" David asked.

"I am not sure."

"Here, give them to me," David asked for binos and took the charge. He scanned the object for a few minutes before suddenly uttering the last word we would've ever wanted to hear – "Pirate ship!"

"What?" almost everyone asked in unison, with a hint of despair.

"Are you sure?" I asked David.

"Yes. There is no naval ID. There is no flag," David said putting away the binos. We all looked at each other's face for a possible solution. Only a few of us had some exposure to previous military and maritime security training. We were not prepared for what was directed our way.

12 p.m.

David, I and Anish stayed on the deck to monitor the supposed pirate ship's movement as it headed our way. Others searched for equipment and devices that might help us in setting up a secure perimetre.

1 p.m.

The crew had collected some daggers, three harpoons, and rescue flairs. We even had a loudspeaker to warn them off. We were on our own. "How close is it?" Sonia asked me.

"It has not moved since. Some twenty miles away."

I then remembered the brief flash on the horizon I had seen last night. "Hey! Everyone," I announced, "I think that ship had been monitoring us since last night. I thought I was imagining, but I saw brief blips of the flashlight from there."

4 p.m.

By 4 p.m, the said ship had not moved from its position. We all stood guard, hoping to defend ourselves with what we had.

"We can seal off the vessel?" asked Sonia. "We'll be safe, simple!" she sought expert approval.

"Not really. If that ship is hostile, they might be loaded with explosives. They can blow up the hatch," David said.

8 p.m.

The pirate ship could not be seen in the dark. It became hard for us to mark its position. We decided to take turns and watch the deck with a night-vision goggle. We were on high-alert until the midnight stuck.

I remember we could not outrun them. Submarines are simply not fast enough. They cannot outrun ships. I prayed for us, "May god be with us."

Day 26

"Fight. Protect. Survive. Win."

12:45 a.m.

Boom! Metal crackling, deafening boom sound, explosion heard. Alarms and sirens went off. We were under the water for a few hours, hoping the ship won't be able to track us. Turns out it neared us in the dark while we were diving the vessel. Pirates attacked us with depth charges (an explosive charge designed to be dropped from a ship or aircraft and to explode under water at a preset depth, used for attacking submarines).

The nightmare finally manifested.

David sounded having traced another depth charge. I remember holding my hands above the head to protect it. Boom! The loudest noise I have ever heard in my life. The charge exploded close to the vessel's upper-open deck. The red blinking light went on and off with the siren. There was the struggle, chaos to preserve our lives. "Control room, now. Go!

Go!" David shouted like mad over the radio. There was smoke in the corridors. I ran behind David, eventually losing his sight in the smoke.

It is a well-known fact that the depth charges do not have to actually hit a submarine to sink it. The shock waves from them, if they even explode within a considerable distance, can tear the metal apart. The immense pressure released makes the water act like a hammer that punches through the underwater submarine. "Sonia, Samira, where are you?" The radio communication was broken. The alarm, the red one was not at all a good sign. It sets-off only when the vessel has a high risk of sinking.

"Here, here!" David appeared from the smoke, turning back, and gave me a hand. "Take the oxygen mask." He gave it to me. I was breathless in the smoke. The smoke was probably from a close by fire due to a damaged electrical board.

"The sealant has broken, the vessel has a massive tear in the wall," Samira's terrified voice came through the loudspeakers. In a few minutes, the crew somehow carried itself together in the control room. We had no other way to surface and move forward!

"How much time before sinking?" Anish asked David and Samira. "About four hours," Samira replied.

"Okay, we surface, move forward, and face this ungodly ship," David proposed. Nobody challenged the decision as time was of the essence.

"Engine full power, tail fins, and elevators up, releasing cabin pressure," David yelled at the top of his voice, the maneuvering procedure of the vessel. A few minutes passed and we surfaced again. "Increase the pump pressure," David shouted again.

We had to remove the collected water to keep the N45 afloat. "Hard turn, crew, hard turn," and he maneuvered the vessel 360 degrees, facing the pirate ship some 800-900 metres away. The pirate ship flashed an orange light in Morse code. It meant, 'Surrender, or we drown.'

"Pump cannot keep up with the water infiltration," Samira said. I saw David trying hard to figure out the last measures. I could sense his helplessness. I could sense the feeling of doom in between my friends. At once, I patted David's shoulder and said, "Head towards the main North Sentinel island."

Day 27

"You wouldn't want to save yourself until it starts burning..."

I was screaming. With every scream, my will to stay alive was fading away. I could see nobody coming to my rescue. It was twenty-one years ago. Our little wooden house had caught fire. I was trapped inside the room, feeling the blanket of fire getting closer with each of my breath. There were people outside my room, scared, troubled, trying to help. Unfortunately, fire is something that has the guts to even overshadow a mother's protective instincts towards her offspring. My mom was certainly not strong. My father was nowhere to be seen. Deep down in my heart, I had accepted the doom approaching me. I was lonely, bound to die this way. I made peace with the supposed painful death by burning alive. Smoke engulfed my lungs, my throat was sour, and I was turning blue due to lack of oxygen. I wished to die by choking rather than burning. It was one of those lowest moments of my human existence when my whole life flashed out in front of the eyes, looking for a possible glimpse of explanation for the current ordeal and possibly death within my memory. Distressful situations are always tricky. Your brain switches to the primitive instincts and acts on its own. It desperately searches for a solution that might work for us, that slightest and faintest chance of our survival. Despite all the courage, intelligence, willpower and innocence, finally, I was about to meet my fate. At the end of my fear of pain, the sorrow of my mom, the screams of my neighbours, my dreams and my very self, stood a benevolent world where I could be free. Free from the burden of existence, and free from the dark side of the world. I was ready. Mentally prepared to unwillingly immolate and submit to the wrath of unforgiving flames. The pain of breathlessness and extreme heat is excruciating. Imagine sitting in a sealed oven topped with hot coals. And it was at that moment when my rescuer came to save my soul. A fireman, with a big helmet, rushed in with a gas mask. All I remember is leaving that burning hell into his arms, and finally opening my eyes in the hospital the next day.

Long loud wails of sirens forced my eyes open. It was noisy. Many alarms and buzzers had gone off together. I could barely see anything. For situational awareness, my mind was totally blank for the next few moments. Treen! Treen! Treen! The fire alarm screamed right above me. It felt a little difficult to breathe. I rubbed my eyes and tried to assess the situation. It was then that I realized that a heavy door was crushing my legs. A chilling pain went through my head. I screamed for help.

'This is it. I got saved from the fire that night. I do not deserve to live. It is now my time' my head constantly broke my will to survive. *C'mon, not now! Where is the crew? Where are we?* All these questions simultaneously struck me. The pirate ship's endless curses hurled at the top of my head. While trying to set myself free from a dead load of a few hundred kilos, my hand caught my radio. I was relieved instantly. But the radio was broken.

Blinking red light bounced off the white smoke and the distress alarms kept me sharp. I took a deep breath and decided to pull my legs with all my might. I was not sure if any or both were broken. Though, this was my only shot. I removed my t-shirt, folded it and held in my mouth. In the case of unbearable pain, I wanted to ensure that I did not bite my tongue off. The first attempt was futile. I couldn't handle the pain. Tears came rolling down my eyes. I kept thinking I was going to die. Though there was something that pushed me off to the limits of pain tolerance. Maybe the idea that my crew needed my help, or the idea that I might not be able to meet my family again, or maybe the mission I was on almost forced me to save myself. I pulled harder and harder, the pain numbed my head for a few seconds, my teeth tore the cloth in my mouth, but I was free in the next few seconds.

I got up against the wall, felt a little dizzy and finally regained the sense of self. At that point, all I could hear was sirens. "David! David!" my frantic voices failed to reach him. No radio, no intercom, no human voices. It seemed like I was the only one left in the stranded vessel. 'Is it sinking?' I thought as I had no idea about the situation. All I remembered was running away from the pirate ship and now this.

I paved my way through fluffy smoke, dragging my hand by the wall, towards the exit. I exited and arrived at the middle deck. Seeping water frightened me to the core. In the unforgiving sea, hostile conditions wouldn't let us survive for more than a few days. "David! Samira! Sonia, Sonia!" I yelled at the top of my voice. My watch said it was 4:12 a.m.

As I dragged my feet forward, the water became deeper and deeper, suggesting that the submarine was inclined. Water was steady though, and I thought, 'Gosh! I think it is stationary, not drowning anymore!' I rushed to the upper level soon after. My only objective now was to find my lost crew. "Anish! Sonia, anyone hear me?" And no response. The treasure chamber was in the lower deck and was probably sunken by now, 'We'll find it again, we know its location,' I thought. The only question bothering me was to know what happened to this vessel in the past few hours.

I went to my room and found it messed up due to the N45's tilt. I immediately grabbed my compact tool-box and hung it around my waist. It had a few tools of help, a medical-aid box, and some flair. 'Never thought I would have to use it,' I thought and took out a few tools and kept it in my left zip pocket. I grabbed the flashlight and went on to search for my friends. The mission room was empty. Notes and papers flew willfully around the room. Pantry, which was usually bustling, was covered with spooky silence.

Somehow, I had a feeling that I was not going to like what I was about to find out. Still, I went on. I moved to the control room. It was half lit due to power outage. My flashlight illuminated the room. As I turned back, I noticed something near the monitors on the far side. I went close to inspect, only to witness the horror I never wanted. It was a trail of blood, starting from the monitors and stretching up to the table's end. It seemed as if somebody was tortured and dragged along that table. My heart was pounding as fast as it could. As the torch illuminated the ground, specks of human blood unraveled themselves. My legs started shaking and tears overflowed as I cried silently in horror. I got myself together and went up to the open deck. I switched off the torch. There it was; the evil shadow of the monster standing in the waking dawn. The pirate ship was a few hundred feet away from the vessel. There, I saw that the main island was hardly a mile away. The thought that my friends had abandoned me faded away after I saw blood. They were in grave trouble, wherever they were. The question was, where was the pirate ship's crew? The nose of the submarine was sunk under the water and the aft-port rose. It appeared to have stuck. An unknown dingy (small boat) stood attached to the N45's starboard side.

I went back in to look for any other trace. As I stepped in, I heard some movement in the upper deck. It was coming from one of the corridors. I stealthily moved towards the source of the sound. A shadow then appeared moving towards me, probably unaware of my presence. It turned out to be Samira. She was startled, but relieved after recognizing me. Her face suddenly turned white with horror, as the man standing behind us hit us with the rifle's butt.

I remember being carried away, half-conscious. They were dragging us and then carried us somewhere else. I remembered hearing a foreign language. I knew we had lost. But I was too weak to fight back, not for my sake, but for Samira. As I soaked in that fallen moment, beep! Beep… beep! Beep! My wristwatch's alarm went off. I fell asleep skipping the memories that followed immediately after that.

Day 28

"If life traps you, survive. Chew-off the trapped paw and survive."

Water drops fell somewhere at a distance. Their sound echoed through my mind. I could hear myself gasping for fresh air. I didn't realize where I was until I noticed some movement above me. A ray of light bounced off my eyes and I was instantly blinded. Footsteps could be heard above my head. I noticed my hands tied behind. There were some sacks beside me, probably wheat. The place was dusty. It was some kind of a storage or cargo hold in an old vessel, probably a steamer. A dim light bulb hung some 10 feet away from me. Its unfocused light caught my attention to a shadow. It was Samira. I could make it out from her distinct brown cargo pants. Though, only her legs were visible. "Samira!" I whispered so as not to alert anyone else. The gravity of the grave danger gripped me instantly. Samira and I had been abducted and were somewhere aboard the pirate ship. I had not found out any trace of other members. David's whereabouts began haunting me. I somehow kept myself from breaking down.

"Samira!" I called her again. There was no response. Occasional footsteps kept me on the guard. I could hear a few men talking. They were talking about some ship or a big underwater boat, and ransom and sometimes a whole different language. They were probably Bangladeshi pirates famous for their notorious activities in the Indian Ocean. 'I don't know how they escaped the Indian navy,' I thought.

Realizing that they were Bangladeshi pirates ignited my deepest fears. In the past three years, these pirates had beheaded several crew members of different nationalities, raped countless women, and looted almost anything they could get their hands on. I feared the worst for my friends, I feared for David. Once you meet the possibility of your own mortality, you no longer remain the same person. I was horrified. Within a blink, my mind switched to survival mode. I began scanning for saving my life, and then Samira's and then move to rescue the rest of the crew.

A sudden strike of a flashlight forced me to close my eyes. I froze as if unconscious. "Let the bitches sleep there," one of the men said before walking away. I rolled right, landed on my knees and stood up silently. That was the moment I had decided that I was not meant to die this way. Deep down within me lay a phoenix with burning wings though I did not realize it until much later.

I walked stealthily towards her and kneeled down beside her. "Samira, hey! Time to go, wake up, Samira," I whispered as I held her head in my arms She was a brave woman, I know that. Samira opened her eyes slowly. I was so relieved. "C'mon, here…get up." I supported her back. We both had suffered concussion due to a blow to our heads. Samira seemed a little dizzy. A few rats ran around squeaking. "We need to get out of here, you hear me. We have to find the rest of the crew," I said.

"Who are they?" she asked as she came over the daze.

"Bangladeshi pirates. I suspect they have captured the crew and kept them somewhere on this ship."

"What about our vessel? N45?" she asked.

I stole my gaze away from her, "N45 is shipwrecked…"

We both began to work on an escape plan. There was only one apparent escape, the cargo doorway above our head. Merely escaping from that chamber would not have sufficed. The pirates were armed with live ammunition. "We need to find a weapon," I proposed. Samira nodded, and we began searching for anything that we could use for self-defense. A few minutes later, we managed to find more bags of grain, some dead rats, a shoe, and a rusted iron rod with a perpendicular nail poking out of its head.

"This might do," Samira said holding the rod. The place was stinking.

The sun had set a few hours before. We could now hear cheers and shouts coming far from the ship's end. It was probably some kind of a celebration… probably the celebration of successfully capturing us. As the sounds grew louder, we hoped to break the doorway and escape. "Wait, where will we go from this ship? N45 is wrecked, right?" Samira asked.

"Yeah…" I pondered for a few seconds. "We will head towards the island. They must have a boat or a dingy. We may even overtake the ship," I said with a streak of over-confidence. Samira did not question my plan. Honestly, we were not in a state to think rationally. As the silence of the dark sea overtook, we began striking the wooden doorway. We kept pushing it, banging it, and striking it with the rod. As soon as we'd hear approaching footsteps, we'd stop. This went on for hours. The cargo hatch did not budge.

Both of us were exhausted, hungry, thirsty, and demotivated. Both of us sat against the sacks, drenched in sweat. Such heavy exercises after a concussion pushed us into uncontrollable sleep. Bright light struck us. I blocked the bright light with my hands, waking up from deep sleep. Somebody was standing on the doorway and watching us. "Here girl, you want some water? Haha." His sinister laugh drove me mad with rage. Though I was still weak and in pain. A stream of water poured down from the gap of the door. I drank it all up. Samira quenched her thirst too.

"Now you want some wine, ladies? Haha," another man came and joined the first one. I remember alcohol poured down from the same place. Both of us were humiliated. The rage inside me grew stronger. We needed a different escape plan.

Day 29

"Even in the face of death, never lose your cool."

As good-natured people always believe the world to be, good-natured like they are, they often become weak when the world around them projects its darkness into their lives. Their mind cannot fathom the extent of evil that prevails. They cannot believe that bad people will hurt them, their loved ones, and their very sense of peaceful existence. To counter that evil and survive, good-natured people must embrace their dark side. It is imperative that they identify their killer instinct, and use it to protect their own interests in the materialistic world.

I woke up abruptly. There was a strong stench, probably of cheap liquor around. I was confused. It was well past midnight. In the stinky cargo chamber of the pirate ship, the only light source for us was that dim bulb. It was illuminated enough for us to identify objects. Yet it wasn't bright enough to see the details of the surroundings. I thought Samira was sleeping until I realized the truth when my eyes adjusted to the poor lighting. She was frozen, as if witnessing a specter. There was a shadow of a man sitting close to her. His rifle's butt bounced-off brown light, kept against the wall behind Samira's back. The man did not realize I was awake. Samira had her vocal chords dead, possibly anticipating what was going to happen to her next.

I was terror-stricken because of the same reason. It was one of the worst things, even worse than death that could possibly happen. The pirate took out his long dagger and began ogling Samira with the cold metal blade. The pointy blade tip touched her forehead, travelled down her neck, chest, before stopping at the navel. I was furious and had made up my mind to lunge at him with force. But, windows of opportunity must be met with preparation. I could feel my right hand trying to grip the rusty iron rod. The bastard pirate was drunk, another blessing in disguise for us. She did not know my action plan. I could sense her shivering with fear.

As the man began digging his face into Samira's neck, I witnessed the darkest animal side of a human being. Her plump body was cold and was paralyzed with fear. He began undressing himself and Samira. As soon as the beastly lust blinded him, I charged his head with the pointy-nail end of the metal rod. In one strike, the nail was driven into his thick skull. I pulled it out and went for another blow to his neck. This time the nail pierced through his neck and a fountain of blood painted the chamber floor and wall red. Samira was in deep shock. I pulled her by the arm and handed over the rod to her. She was so receptive at that time that she did not even think twice before striking that pervert pig herself. The half-dead pirate was completely dead as Samira's strike punctured his eye and drove the nail through his brain.

In a fit of rage, anger, humiliation, terror, and complex thoughts, Samira repeatedly struck the pirate's lifeless body with the rod until his skin spurted blood from multiple punctures. I had to stop her to make sure no unwanted attention was attracted. My gaze came across my watch. I lit the screen. It was 3:30 a.m. Some movement could be heard on the deck. We had to hide the body quickly. "Hey! Give me a hand," I said as I pulled the legs to drag the body away. She kept looking at the man's disfigured face. "Samira!" I shouted. She automatically grabbed his torso and we hid the body behind a bunch of grain sacks. I covered the visible blood on the floor with a piece of cloth from the pirate's dead body.

What a dark minute that was. We both sat down to contemplate. My mind was racing fast. We were far-off from our original mission. It was out of the question for now. The crew was missing. N45 was partially sunk. However, the cargo doorway was now unlocked. And… I spotted the heavy assault rifle that stood against the wall.

Day 30

"If you aim to win, know how a tiger hunts and the stag evades."

Last time I had picked up a rifle was years ago. It was during the naval diving course when I had a chance to blow up a few cardboard targets with a sniper rifle. Today was a question of life and death. I was holding a loaded 'Thompson' submachine gun or SMG as they call it. Samira had come to senses. Ten hours had passed since that pervert was sent to hell for the judgment. "They'll be here soon," I whispered in Samira's ear.

"It has been hours. Nobody came looking for him," she said.

"They haven't realized that he is missing, yet! It can be anytime soon. I want you to do exactly what I say. You understand?" Samira nodded in affirmation.

"What next?" she asked.

Both of us were lying on the floor close to each other, monitoring every movement and sound on the deck.

"We do not know their strength. They can be ten or a hundred. We will stealthily escape from the hatch as the sun sets. Let us wait for them to get drunk again. I hope others are close by. We will look for them once we are out. You will keep an eye on any boat or raft that can help us escape," I explained.

"Sounds like a plan," she said.

"We have only one shot. If we're compromised, we're dead," I said while looking into her eyes. Samira was scared at first, but put her brave face on soon.

12:10 a.m.

"I think they are retreating inside for drinking. There must be a few on the deck for the night watch," I said. "Here, take this," and I threw the metal rod into her hands. "Stay right behind me, Samira." I instructed her. She nodded again, like a child listening to her mommy. I covered the dim light bulb with a cloth to conceal any shadow movements. Someone instantly walked past our place without noticing anything suspicious. We sighed in relief. "Wait for them to get drunk," I said. And then was a seemingly endless wait of another twenty minutes, the pirates retreated back. Their voices eventually grew louder signifying that their routine celebration had begun.

"On my mark, just follow me and keep your eyes open. Remember, do not scream or shout. Be ready to take action," I tried to give Samira the last-minute brief. We stood up. I held the rifle in my right hand, and slowly pushed the wooden hatch by a few inches. My eyes could scan the upper deck partially. Nobody was present in sight. Suddenly, I remembered some tools that I had retained during the initial search. The pirates took away my box, but some tools were still left with me. My hand fumbled inside the pocket and got hold of a small key. This key was meant to connect sockets of screws with the drivers of different sizes. I took it out and threw it with force on the upper deck. There was a noticeable *tuck tuck* sound of metal striking the wood followed by rolling noise. A few seconds passed and no movement was registered. The window of opportunity was clear.

With the slightest possible movement, I raised myself up to the deck and held a crawling position. "Give me your hand." I pulled Samira up. Every second of vigilance paid off. Nobody had noticed us until then. Both of us crawled for the next 30 feet or so and got a cover behind the tall mast. Noises came from the large cabin some 40 feet behind us. Shadows of men partying and drenched in alcohol shone through the lit cabin windows.

I crawled further towards what I thought was another hatch. "Stay right behind me," I whispered to Samira. Her eyes were fixed at a point above my head. The look on her face growing pale was evident in the bright moonlight. "What do you see?" I asked her. Holding the rifle and movement constraints kept me from directly looking up. "Hey, what is it?" I whispered again. Samira's eyes grew bigger and the terror on her face was as clear as the night sky.

What we witnessed that night was the epitome of barbarism. It is one thing that I wish could be unseen. There was a human head, on the ship's railing, wedged to a spear.

A puppy runs towards its mother and the pack upon sensing the blood of a close relative. We did the same. Samira and I locked ourselves in the hatch. We had a lot to process in. I fell into her arms, sobbing like a child. I feared the same treatment for others. We were stuck in a cage where the inhumane barbarians decided our left-out days. We began the countdown for our lives.

Day 31

"The Judgment Day..."

Sun rays hit my eyes and woke me up. I was still shaking. The human head had haunted me all night. Samira's shock probably wore off, as she slept drooling close to a grain sack. I suddenly caught sight of footsteps approaching the hatch. I quickly hid the rifle behind a sack. The hatch was lifted and two ugly men came down. "Give them the food, otherwise the bitches will die. If they are weak, master won't be able to enjoy them... haha," one of them said in a sinister tone. I folded my legs in my arms and tried not to make eye contact with them. They threw a few pieces of bread for me and Samira. One of them sat close to me. "You from America?" he asked in broken English. I chose not to respond and looked away.

"Hehe, you got pride. You are beautiful. Your country is proud too. It does injustice to weak country. That is why we arrest you. Master will talk to your government. No ransom, no live. You will be our slave forever...haha," and he began groping me. I resisted but couldn't do much to overpower him. His partner then said, "C'mon. We have other dogs to feed too."

They left and shut the hatch down. Their visit made one thing clear. They had other 'dogs' to feed. Some, if not all, crew members were alive. Hopes got higher and I wished to see Sonia, David, and Anish soon. But we had to survive. I woke Samira up. "Listen! We are ambushing the bastards." She woke up rubbing her eyes. I could see the haunted look in her eyes as the darkness of last night's incident still sent cold shivers down our spines.

"Wait, what?" asked Samira.

"Yes, an ambush Samira. That is the only way to take them down. We cannot be stealthy. You saw what they did to him! Here, grab it!" I threw the iron rod to her. "Same rules, stay behind me." I rechecked the rifle and tried mimicking the aim a few times. Meanwhile, the hidden dead body had started stinking. "Either way, we won't survive here for long," I said to her.

"What is your guess on their number?" she asked me.

"Well, judging by the noise and footsteps I have counted so far, they should be around fifteen strong." I got up and searched the dead pirate's foul smelling body for some more ammunition. I found an extra Thompson mag in his jacket. "Cool, some more firepower," I said to myself and kept the mag in my pocket.

"You have limited rounds, use them wisely," Samira advised. I nodded in agreement and looked right in her eye. "It is time." She nodded, and we broke open the hatch. Broad daylight revealed us in front of some five pirates working on the deck.

I aimed the rifle, took stance on my hip, and pressed the trigger. *Boom boom boom, thud thud thud, kachick, boom boom*

boom! I ripped the rifle's muzzle open and it spat fire all around. Three pirates succumbed to my bullets. One escaped. I started firing in bursts. The bullets were glazed with lead and were of heavy caliber. Flying chunks of wood and metal stated the penetration power of each of it. The rifle mercilessly took down the running pirate.

The adrenaline rush slowed and I noticed. It had only been a few seconds. "C'mon!" I signalled Samira to follow me and look for the rest of the crew. Other pirates were on to us the next moment. As we ran, I asked Samira to collect all the ammunition she could from the dead pirates. She briefly searched for two bodies and grabbed a pistol and some magazines. Both of us took cover on the bow side of the ship. We began screaming the crew's name, but it didn't make any difference then. We were running out of time. The crew must have already heard the action on the deck. Amidst the exchange of the bullets, I heard a voice calling me. "Donna! Donna!" I recognized it without any doubt. It was David.

"David! Where are you?" I shouted while aiming at the stern side. Soon, the deck was covered in a layer of salt-pepper and gunpowder smoke.

"We are in the cellar right beneath you," David yelled.

"Samira, cover me," I shouted. Samira was now in her killer mode. Each bullet she fired was deadly accurate and hit the hostile bodies. She killed and maimed four bastards on the stern side. Just as I began scanning the floor beneath my foot, a bullet graze momentarily disabled my left shoulder. My Thompson SMG fell down. *Crap*, I thought as I struggled to regain my stance. I continued to scan the ground for a hatch or cellar opening and grabbed back the rifle again. Seconds later, I found it. "Samira, you won't be able to hold them back with the pistol. Here, take the rifle and buy me some time, I've found them," I yelled as I threw the SMG towards her.

"Got it, but I can't hold them for much longer. I'll need close support ASAP," She shouted from the other side.

"Hang in there tight!" I said to her as I lifted the latch with all my strength. There they were; Sonia, David, and Anish waiting for my arrival and ultimately their chance to survive. The group was united again.

"Take cover! Move… move… move…" David hassled out Sonia and Anish.

"Grab whatever you can, to defend yourself. David, we need to deboard the ship ASAP," I said to him. He looked into my eyes and nodded in affirmation.

"Hey! Cover me," Samira shouted.

"Here is a raft, Donna. David, help me lower it in the waters," Samira placed the last piece of the puzzle, key to our survival. I grabbed the Thompson and salvaged a few magazines. I covered the crew with bursts of hot lead as they lowered the boat.

There were a few pirates still left. I don't know if we got their leader. But it was time to leave the ghastly ship. As I crossed the railing, once again, the severed head stared right at me. Beneath it hung a note which I had not seen before. It read *All traitors shall meet their fate.*

A moment of confusion and I disembarked on the raft with the rest of the crew. Sporadic shots pierced the sea water around our small wooden raft. I covered us with the last few rounds in my hand. Sonia, Anish, David, and Samira rowed as hard as they could. "Head towards the island," David shouted. The main Sentinel island was our last resort. The island grew closer as the haunting pirate ship grew smaller.

Ahead of us, we had a new world; an unknown island. Our mission was long lost. As soon as the raft touched the beach sand, we ran blindly towards the island, away from death. Tall trees greeted us on the land. The beach was around 300-400 metres wide. And beyond that stood a densely packed forest. I kneeled down and all others fell straight on the white sand. Sun rays, salt and island breeze had taken us into its protective shelter. At a seemingly safe spot, I fell asleep instantly.

Day-32

"Camping all the way..."

It was a cold night. Five of us had been on the run. Whatever could possibly go wrong had gone wrong with us. N45 had partially sunk; we could see its red light on a mile away from us. The damned pirate ship still retained its stance. It too hadn't budged since we deboarded it. Its shadow against the horizon told us that the danger had not been mitigated; it had just been delayed. The sand was our comfort tonight. David and Anish were busy trying to light a fire.

We were drenched, salt and sand had chafed our skin. Yet it was not something we would have complained about at the time. Samira, Sonia and I desperately waited for the sun to rise. Daylight is always encouraging. It holds a mysterious power to inject hope in the most fragile souls. The island was eerily quiet. A few feet from where we sat, David and Anish succeeded in sparking the twigs. Crackles of burning wood and local vegetation soon mixed with the serene land breeze. It was a cocktail enough to ease the distress and shock we all had just been through.

Everyone was too tired to discuss anything, speak or express anything. It seemed that we were celebrating our lives once again, in person, in complete solitude. David settled himself beside me, falling asleep without any word. Sonia and Anish took a guarding stance and volunteered to keep a watch on the shore and the forest. I kept gazing the fearless campfire.

As silence and contemplation engulfed all of us, one thing kept bothering me. The note I saw beneath the severed head. Why did they kill him? And not any of us? Crackles of the burning twigs grew intense. There is something that we are missing, something that I cannot see. My mind raced against time. The pirates attacking a heavy submarine with a mid-sized ship was not brave. They seemed overconfident. If they had crossed our path coincidentally, they would not have attacked us on just a whim. They had depth charges, a precise weapon to drown a submarine. There was no way the pirates did not know about us beforehand. 'They surely 'smelled' the treasure,' I thought. But how? And with a plethora of questions and brainstorm, I decided to sleep. My body needed rest. I rubbed ashes from the campfire onto my graze wound and fell asleep.

Day 33

"Unfamiliar situations are the best teachers for life."

"The pirates haven't budged since forever," David said staring at the pirate ship. It was hardly a mile-and-a-half away from the island, and the N45 stood wrecked close to it.

"Well! What now, any plans, suggestions, anyone?" Sonia asked. I was walking bare feet on the sand, to and fro. That is usually my way of figuring things out.

"We need to find a better shelter, probably build a defense line to keep them from coming here. The sun is already out. Pirates might come ashore anytime," said Anish.

"How much ammunition do we have?" Samira asked me.

"Thirty something SMG bullets… What about your pistol?" I asked her while reloading the Thompson.

"Twelve," she said.

We sighed, and then Sonia said, "Maybe we can carve out some hand-held weapons, at least as a last resort." We initially disregarded the idea. But, Sonia's idea could have been an effective shot. Something is still better than nothing.

"Donna! Give me the SMG," David asked. I handed the rifle to him.

"What we can do is set up a camp somewhere deep in the forest. Our priority is to evade the pirates. We can then plan our great escape, and possibly retrieve our treasure from the sub," Anish proposed.

"Treasure is the last priority, Anish; you still think we are thinking about that chest?" Samira was losing it.

Before the discussion turned hot, I intervened, "Let's build a camp first, we will plan further from there. And, use every bullet wisely."

"Do we have any communication equipment, satellite phone maybe?" Sonia asked as she continuously brainstormed for a solution. I could sense her fright. Still, she was a tested problem-solver and her positive attitude was speaking loudly at that time. We all looked for anything that could help us establish contact with the outside world.

"I remember the satellite phone was in the mission room. I mean that is where I remember it to be," Samira said. We began marching deep into the island's forest.

"Hey, Samira, how badly do you think N45 is damaged? I mean would it still have some systems running?" I asked.

"I guess so, did not get a chance to run diagnosis, hehe.... but yeah, a few electrical systems should be alive," she said as we paved our way through the exotic leafy vegetation of that magnificent ecosystem. I looked around. The distant chirping of birds, giant wildflowers, high-hanging fruits, and a few tree-jumping monkeys eased the air. Sentinel island was a different world.

"Eventually, we will have to return to our vessel. N45 still has months of the food supply, communication, and medical aids," said David.

We had been walking for the last fifteen minutes. We were deep inside the jungle. Tall dense tropical trees barred the sunlight from touching the ground. A somewhat plain spot which seemed easier to clean became our campsite. The crew utilized its afternoon building shelters, carving spears, collecting wood fire, some fruits, and a secure perimetre around the campsite. The sun was sleepy and was soon going to lie down. After a long time, I was feeling protected again. We settled across each other around the bonfire. Our site was at a decent distance from the coast, so our fire was virtually untraceable. Detecting smoke at night was also next to impossible.

"I don't think they'll follow us here. We can easily overpower them here." David pacified the team. "Our best shot is to regain control of N45, grab the communication equipment and call in for rescue," David said as he drank from the green coconut. We agreed unanimously.

Darkness prevailed and the island once again screamed with silence. The campfire burnt with all its might. I threw in a couple of chopped fire woods, thanks to my spare tools. I took a few sips from David's coconut before falling asleep in his arms "We will make it, Donna." He reassured me. I nodded in full confidence. "I mean not just live, we will retrieve what is ours. We have paid enough," he said. His words cautioned me against any rash decision he might be making. But, he made sense. We had paid enough. There was no looking back now. I slept on David's left arm, and the SMG gun slept on his right arm.

Day 34

"New morning, new hopes..."

"Chop some more woods, looks like it might rain," Anish told David. It was cloudy that day and a thunderstorm seemed close to the coast. The crew was scattered in the camp vicinity. Some collecting eatables and others strengthening the shelter.

"Hey, David! Shall we take a look at the coast?" I asked.

"No, it's too risky," he replied as he continued to chop the wood.

"I was thinking if we can get a fresh picture of the scenario. We'll be in stealth." I sat close to him and tried making my point.

He pondered for a second and said, "Okay. Take Samira with you." I nodded in affirmation and called Samira. My idea was to take a look at the coast and gain some situational awareness. I patted Samira on her shoulders and we began our march to the coast.

It was a twenty-minute walk from our campsite deep inside the tropical forest. We traced back our initial track.

"I…I… I can't forget his head, Donna," Samira opened up about her feelings. "It makes me feel sick." I stopped her, turned her back by the shoulder and gave her a tight hug.

"I am with you, Samira. We will make it through. Trust me," I said without anything to support my beliefs.

"I trust you," she said crying a little.

"You know what, that treasure is seemingly becoming yummier…haha." I joked and it worked. She smiled a little and we continued our walk.

"So what are we looking for?" Samira asked.

"I don't know. Just wanted to see if that ungodly ship has moved, maybe a boat, vessel nearby, I don't know," I murmured casually.

The coast appeared in the next few minutes. I could never miss the sound of distant sea waves. "Stay low buddy, we cannot reveal our position," I instructed.

"Got it," she replied.

Both of us ducked behind some tall trees that easily concealed our bodies. The pirate ship and the N45 were at the same place.

"Why hasn't it moved?" Samira asked with a hint of frustration.

"I don't know. Maybe because we killed the captain, haha." I joked.

"You know your humour is getting darker, right?" she reflected on me.

I did ponder on that. Maybe my humour *is* twisted. "They did not kill any of us, they wanted us for something. They still want something from us. I don't think they are going anywhere. What say?" I said.

"Maybe they are after the treasure. But if that is the case, how did they know about it? And Donna, how do we open N45's treasure vault?" Samira asked me after stumbling upon a worthwhile doubt.

"Uh... PIN code. The chamber's vault is secured by a PIN code. Maybe the treasure chamber is drowned, but the only way to recover it is the... PIN... Oh my god!" I was shocked and fascinated. "They want to know the password from us," I exclaimed. "And only three of us know it," I gazed at her. David, I and Anish were the only ones who knew the drowned vault's passcode.

The pirates apparently did not kill us because the vault's pin was still to be extracted. Maybe they would have tortured each of us. But time outsmarted their evil plan.

Day 35

"Best views wait for us behind the ugly present... do they?"

"Have you ever felt that you are trapped in a cage, screaming your pain out, crying for help, but the helping hands just fly away? Have you ever been there? Tolerance is a subjective topic. We can only bear so much pain we are designed for. Not the physical pain, torturous soul piercing pain, the mental pain. You can counsel me all you want. You can motivate me all you want. Yes, I can see the light at the end of all of this. But I know the truth, far uglier truth. The light seems to move two steps away as you move two steps toward it. I can see it, but I also know I will never find it. You might label it as depression or anxiety, but the truth is...it is absolute reality. Call me a pessimist, a nihilist. I think there are only a few things worth living for. And, once they are gone, your existence begins haunting you. That is human life. That is my life," I remember my speech for the shrink. She was my appointed counselor after I was diagnosed with

clinical depression. "You see my point here, Donna," she said in a humble empathetic tone, "The world is not fair. There are bad things out there. Even life isn't fair. But we are creatures of passion. To swim through fires and survive the most baffling laws of nature is what makes us unique. Not the talent, not the money, not the fame, but the will that lies somewhere deep inside your heart. You won't see it because you are too fixated on the light moving away from you. Helping yourself does not mean making sense of the external world as it is. It is to self-reflect and to learn. Learn and keep moving. Learn and keep moving, learn and keep moving..."

I almost woke up soaked in sweat. My hands felt the warm island sand. The campfire had died out hours ago. Traces of white smoke from the ashes greeted me first. It was a fairly sunny day. I looked around. Sonia was sitting beside me, shaving a wooden spear with a stone.

"Both the guys are off exploring the island. Here, take this." She threw a cracked coconut at me. I caught it subconsciously.

"Thanks." I smiled at her. I got up with the coconut in one hand, wiped the sand off my clothes and stretched my body. "Where is Samira?" I asked.

"I don't know, she was here just a few minutes back," Sonia replied.

"Did she walk to the coast?"

"Think so," she replied.

'She must be gauging the ships. Samira wouldn't have reached, I can catch her if I run,' I thought to myself. "Hey Sonia, I am gonna take a look at her. Tell the guys when they return." Sonia nodded as she sharpened the spear.

I began walking down the usual path to the coast. My estimate said she shouldn't be more than a minute away from me. As I cut through the light bushes and exotic island flora, I caught sight of her walking down the trail. She did not notice me. I had a plan in my mind. Stealthily, I sneaked behind her. "Boo!" I scared her. Samira was startled, losing complete balance and falling on one side of the trail. I grabbed her hand. She looked frightened.

"You… Donna, this isn't funny," she said.

"That was not funny at all." She couldn't be more right, and I could not stop laughing. I picked her up. "Walking down to pirates, all alone?" I asked.

"Just a stroll, wanted to see what has changed," Samira replied. We continued to walk.

"Well, I'd advise that none of us be alone, especially when we are trapped amidst dangers." I casually advised her.

"Ah, the waves!" she exclaimed. The coast was close.

We covered ourselves behind thick vegetation and trees. What we saw was probably one of the most frightening sights of our adventure. What we thought was left behind stood before us. "Oh my god, Jesus!" We both exclaimed in unison. The pirate ship stood at the coast, anchored. It was only a few hundred feet from us.

"We are in some serious trouble now," I said.

"Shh… let us see if there is any movement," Samira said.

As we scanned the pirate ship, I felt a strange sensation. It was as if we were already surrounded, but did not know about it. I think I heard leaves crackling, sand gravels crushing, a few feet on both the sides. I scanned the space around us. I saw nothing.

"There is no movement on the ship," Samira said, "That means only two things. Either they are deboarding and coming for us, or.... they are already inside the jungle."

We were both paralyzed by the horrific ways this encounter might end. We had limited protection and ammunition as well.

"Hurry, we need to get to the campsite, now!" I said.

We rushed back to the 'hole' like a rabbit speeding away from the fox. Upon reaching the campsite, Samira and I were out of breath. "Hey! What is up with you two?" Anish asked piling up the firewood.

"The pirate ship has reached the coast," Samira said.

"What?? Damn it!" David said.

"We don't know if they have already infiltrated into the island," I said. A few moments passed as we all dug into our survival and problem-solving instincts.

"We must move up into the jungle. We need to buy time," said David.

"Hmm, but for how long will we keep running?" Anish raised a doubt.

"I don't know. For now, this is the only possible solution. We cannot face them with thirty something bullets. That would be the last resort." David made his point. We all agreed. "Alright, time to move, let's get going deeper into the island," David instructed us.

Within the next few minutes, the crew packed all the firewood, food, and belongings. We marched deeper into the jungle, hoping that the pirates would not be able to easily trace us. David tore apart a fiber from a climbing plant and tied a long wooden stick to it. He made three such arrangements. "Okay!

We need to hide our trail. No footprints mean no traceability. The members walking behind will drag these wooden logs with them to erase any traces on the soil." His plan sounded brilliant. We did not question its effectiveness.

The team marched for about an hour. "We have probably covered 8 miles or so. This seems like a dense spot. Probably the island's centre," Anish said.

"Let us set up the camp here and secure the perimetre," said David.

We erected the camp again. Our eyes gazed the campfire in the evening, hoping that we would survive this ordeal. We, the treasure hunters, had now become fugitives on an unknown island.

Day 36

*"There are no demons under the bed.
There are demons outside."*

The night passed away peacefully. At least we did not wake up to gunpoint. It was 6:00 a.m. Our campfire had not extinguished and was spewing white smoke. "Hey put that out, you don't want them to get here." David filled the hot pit with sand. The smoke vanished. Our perimetre kept us safe in the night.

"We need to collect some fruits and edible vegetation," Sonia said.

"This is what early nomadic ancestors would have felt like, only we are experiencing it much faster," I pointed.

"Seems so," Sonia said.

"Hey, Donna," David called me from a distance, "Where is Samira?"

"I don't know," I said. I asked Sonia.

"Haven't seen her in a while. I thought she had gone to take a leak in that direction." She pointed towards the direction which we had come from.

"When did she wake up?" I asked.

"Around four in the morning," Sonia replied with uncertainty.

It was weird. Samira never takes long. Though, wandering off was kind of her habit. 'Let us wait for a few more minutes. She might be returning. She cannot be lost, the path is well defined,' I thought.

We ate and began discussing our plan to stay alive. It was 6:30 and Samira's absence was now noticeable. "Where is she, girls?" Anish asked. We were growing impatient.

"Let us check, we'll be right back," I said and left with Sonia to know Samira's whereabouts. "She is acting weird since yesterday, have you noticed?" I wanted Sonia's view.

"Maybe, I am not sure. Let us blame it on the circumstances," she said.

We searched the perimetre, 200 metres in all the directions from the campsite. No sign of Samira. Tension began surfacing amidst the team soon.

"When is the last time anybody saw her?" David asked.

"I saw her waking up at around 4," Sonia said. Apparently, nobody had seen her except Sonia that morning.

David sighed. "Okay, remember, nobody gets left behind. Look for her in all directions. We cannot move the camp without her," he said. "Look for her in pairs, not alone."

Three hours had passed. No traces of her were found. Not even footprints. I was searching for her with Sonia. Anish and David met us as we circled back to the campsite. David stood with his hands on the waist, "Anything?"

"No," replied Sonia, bending on her knees to relax for a while.

I drank some coconut water we had preserved. The island was humid and dehydration was possible. "Do you think they kidnapped her?" I raised a valid suspicion.

"I don't think so. They would have captured all of us," Sonia said.

"But Samira knows the vault's password, right?" Anish said in a flow.

It wasn't until the next minute when I realized that something sinister was going on. We were blind and weak to see it through. 'How did Anish know that pirates are looking for the vault's password? It was something I had discussed with Samira the other day,' I thought. I began stitching the events together. Some pieces were missing. But for now, Samira was my concern, and so I ignored Anish. Possibly another big irreversible mistake I made on the North Sentinels.

"Let us look for her once again. We have to move, we don't have time," David said. We parted ways to look for our beloved friend. I noticed how Anish was carrying the Thompson SMG and not David. It worried me a little. Anish was coming off as fishy to me.

A few more hours of the operation yielded no results. Samira was lost somewhere in the deep jungle, without any trace. It was a scary moment for us. How could she just disappear into thin air? I realized the presence of an invisible sinister force lurking the crew. Something was on to us. And, it was not the pirates, I had a hunch.

David, Sonia and I reluctantly packed up the camp and began migrating forward. "God, keep our beloved friend Samira safe," Sonia prayed. Our footsteps followed the jungle trail further.

"We will find her," David pacified us. We had no option but to hope for the best and be prepared for the worst.

Day 37

"If sleep doesn't come easily, you are too close to the goal... or death."

I woke up to loud voices. David and Anish were arguing over something. "We can't live here forever; we have to get back to N45." David grew louder.

"And do what?? Tell me… you will do what then?" Anish was defensive.

"Hey, hey! What's the matter?" I woke up, rubbing my eyes.

"The island's other end is close. We have no other choice than going back to the vessel. We need to call for help," David said.

"What if the communication equipment is down?" Anish objected.

"You are being weirdly pessimistic, Anish. You don't want to live? What has gotten into you?" I was puzzled and angry at him.

"Going back there is risking our lives for no good reason, why don't you understand?" He kept obstructing our will to head back to the vessel.

Sonia came into the scene soon. "What's the matter with you all?" I explained the scene to her.

"Anish, what do you propose? How do we survive?" Sonia questioned him intensely.

"I am not dying with you guys. I am out of here." He stayed clear of any explanation. The three of us were perplexed regarding his behaviour.

Suddenly, we heard a familiar voice. It was another surprise, more of a shock. The static noise came from one of Anish's pockets. The noise came from a radio set. Our eyes were set on him. Clearly, something was going on, hidden from us all along. For a moment, everything froze. Four of us kept exchanging looks with each other. All fears were about to manifest themselves. I noticed the SMG in Anish's hand.

"Whatever you have in mind, put that SMG down, Anish. Let's remain calm. We need to get out of here alive, in one piece," I said slowly approaching him. It was in the blink of an eye before we could realize what happened, and Anish had the rifle pointed at me.

"You better back off, lady. You don't know what is going on here. It's been a while… 'playing friends'! You freaks will do as I say." Anish revealed his true colours.

"What, for god's love, is this Anish?" David said in utter confusion. My puzzle of suspicion was almost complete.

"Where is Samira?" I asked him. Honestly, I wasn't scared of Anish's little game. He thought for a moment, "I have got nothing to do with those idiots." He gloated again, "I am on a different mission," he said.

"What's up with the radio set?" I asked.

"Nothing to do with you," said Anish.

The three of us had our brains plagued with distrust and questions. Reality itself was in question. I couldn't tell true from false, up from down. Still, my face hid my fear well. "Here is what you three ducks will do. You will pick up this camping and keep moving. We have a treasure to find," Anish said.

"So this is what it is all about! The treasure?" I couldn't digest his ulterior motive.

"Don't try to understand things beyond your comprehension, lady," he said moving the barrel closer to me. "Move your asses now, we're losing daylight."

David and I made eye contact with each other. I reached one conclusion. Fort Bridge Corp was somehow involved in this mess. I didn't know how. But I was certain. "Is Fort Bridge behind you, my friend?" I asked boldly.

Anish ignored. "Keep moving. We have miles to go," he said poking my back with the SMG's barrel.

We kept moving deeper into the jungle. My soul was getting crushed with frustration. Everyday something was going wrong and I had no control. Now this backstabber Anish wanted us to find the treasure. God knew what else he had in mind and what lengths he was willing to go.

The half-hour of frustrating walk came to a halt. "Set up the camp here. Anybody who tries to outsmart me will get their head filled with hot lead." Anish threatened us. I could almost hear someone else talking from inside him. It seemed like a demonic possession. That's how unbelievable it was. "Quick! Set up the fire! We have a lot to do in very less time." We became submissive and did as he pleased. David, Sonia and I constantly looked at each other helplessly, waiting for a window of opportunity to strike.

That night

The fire burnt brightly as always. As I gazed at its core, I felt a warm, cozy feeling fleeting through my forehead. It was the only sense of security I had at the time, and David. Three of us sat on one side of the fire, hands tied, and anything dangerous taken away. Anish, the moron, sat opposite to us. The rifle rested between his legs, with the barrel pointing at the stars. He kept looking in our eyes like a maniac.

"What are you staring at?" Sonia lost her temper.

Anish smirked. "You three have always been the strong ones. Others were weak," he began speaking.

"What have you done to Samira?" David asked.

"She was just another little girl." Anish said polishing the barrel with his shirt. "She probably got lost or died… of her own stupidity," he said.

"Why are you doing this Anish?" I asked, restoring my calm with a mighty effort.

"You had a mission. It failed. I have my own mission. Simple," Anish replied.

"What mission?"

"The treasure, dear Donna. Only you three can find it. We are close to it. I know that," he said while gazing at the fire probably, contemplating his puny existence.

"We are compromised. The pirates are behind us, N45 is down. How will we find it?" I asked.

"You will do it. You have no other option. Fort Bridge will let you out only when you find the treasure. If you fail, there are enough bullets and enough land to bury your worthless bodies, haha." He threw that annoying smirk once again.

"So you are Fort Bridge's rat! Who's your master, rat?" David ground his teeth.

"Does it make a difference? Whoever he/she is, both of us are going to get rich soon. And, that is beneficial for you too. You get to live," said Anish.

"All that time, all those moments, all fake, a masquerade, you cheat!" Sonia yelled at Anish.

"People come and go, darling. In between, they change. Donna's foolishness led me aboard the N45. I wasn't expecting it."

"Why not play along? Why not work as a team and take equal share home?" I asked.

"Well, I don't like to share. You would have run away from the pirates without even looking for the Nizam's treasure. I could have destroyed the old piece of floating crap, that pirate ship, in a moment. Fort Bridge has got some serious juice with them. Yesterday, however, they grew impatient. And, honestly, I too want to see the treasure now." Anish sauntered all night around the campfire, talking over the radio every few hours. Sonia, David and I were like the mice trapped in a corner. Do or die were the only options with us. Samira's whereabouts were still unclear. My heart screamed for help. Yet, the island was haunted with silence.

Day 38

"Sometimes dreams walk to you themselves, not in the happy hour."

5:00 a.m.

"Wake up guys," Anish poked my and Sonia's back with the gun as we slept. While you are asleep, waking up to the barrel of a gun can be one haunted alarm. "Time to go fishin' ladies, and wake him up too!" Anish pointed at David as he walked away, pulling the radio set closer to his mouth. Sonia looked at me like an angry little girl. I stared at her so as to indicate her to keep her cool.

"What is he going to do!" she whispered. I looked away nodding negatively.

5:45 a.m.

The evil man did not even untie our hands. We struggled with our morning natural calls. It was the hour of embarrassment. "You can at least untie us for a few minutes." I was losing my cool. He kept ignoring my plea.

"We are ladies, you moron," Sonia yelled at him.

Anish suddenly confronted her, looking like a beast into Sonia's innocent and scared eyes. He closed in on her and it looked like he was about to raise his manly hands on her.

"Big man you are!" David came in. "Go ahead, do what you want to do to her. You'll be losing your manhood without gelding, haha!" David kept poking the monster until Sonia was safe, and David himself became the target. Anish landed a terribly powerful punch on David's face. I haven't felt that helpless before. It was like a punch to me. I shivered with silent shrieks of cry. My eyes filled with tears.

David carried himself back up. "You got a terrible punching style, mate, haha." David was being stupid now. "You punch like a little girl," he said to Anish. The cold-hearted Anish punched David in the guts.

"Stop it, you monster!" I screamed. I tried to kick him. My attempts went in vain. Amidst all this, the radio set spoke loudly, "404 coming in. What the status?" a hoarse voice articulated from the other side. Anish's attention shifted to the radio set and he walked a few yards away. Three of us kept exchanging looks, breathing heavily.

5:55 a.m.

"I've had enough of you," Anish grinned at us. It looked like someone had grilled him good over the radio. But it was no good news for us. "The three of you are going to do what I say. You, come here," he said grabbing David by his collar and dragging me by the arm. Anish then tied another knot to Sonia's hand and covered her mouth with a handkerchief.

"What do you want?" I asked.

He hurried and ignored me.

Anish then kneeled Sonia down, pointed the SMG at her head. As she shivered and cried for her life, he said, "You two fools listen to me. This lovely friend of yours is alive, breathing, and peeing in her pants. To save her, you just have to follow my words." He kept talking like the psycho from the *American Psycho* movie. "Both of you will head back to the beach. You will dive into the ocean. You'll find a few caverns. Some of them open back into the island. In one of those caverns, the Nizam's Treasure is hidden. You just have to tell me which one it is. Understood?" I and David locked eyes at him.

"Why do you think the treasure is here?" David asked.

"Well, you're not the only researcher here. I have read Donna's notes. She knows the three possible spots where the treasure can be. It has to be." Anish winked at me.

"You..." I grinned. David asked me to stay back. "Why don't you search it for yourself and let us go. We won't tell," I said to him.

"Don't try to play smart, lady. How would I know if you are telling me the truth, or planning to overpower me? Think before you speak," his arrogant mouth kept mumbling.

"If you fail to find the treasure or try to display your smartness in any manner, I will decorate the sand here with Sonia's insides." Anish's threat sent chills down my spine.

"Why don't you keep her out of this?" David intervened, "We can use her. She can assist us in the dives and your job will be done quickly."

"Awww! You same old David. It is so you." Anish grinned and smiled, "You really think I have you three begging me because I am a fool? I took you for being wise. Sonia isn't going anywhere," he said. As we dealt with her hostage situation, Sonia seemed to have fallen into the trap of hopelessness. I could hear her murmuring chants from the Bible. Didn't know she was a religious soul.

"What about the pirates? They are behind us." I pointed it out to the moron in case he was missing it.

"They are gone!" he said.

"We will need equipment to dive," David said.

"Now don't be unreasonable, you two," said Anish with an exasperation. "I've seen you dive without snorkels and cylinders. Just locate the goddam treasure and get it over with," he said.

"This is ocean water. We dove without equipment in inland waters," I said while secretly trying to untie my hands.

"Don't make it harder than it is, you little bitch." Anish screamed in frustration. "We are heading back to the coast, you both are diving or this lady's brain will be decorating your faces. Move now!" Anish's coerce tactics were working pretty well. There was nothing at the moment we could have done.

7:07 a.m.

More than an hour of walk led us to the coast; same old waves hitting the shore. I noticed the spot where I and Samira had come two days ago for the recon. Her memory made me weak. I couldn't stop my tears thinking of her fate. 'Poor Samira. Where are you?' I kept thinking of her. And now Sonia's fate was at stake because of this backstabber psycho. It was a lot to process, a lot to digest. I asked Anish, "How much are you being paid? Did you get paid to kill her as well? Do you like killing innocent people for your greed?" He stared at me and I did the same. I could see rage in his eyes. I bet he could see the same in mine.

We came closer to the beach. He knelt Sonia down. "You two stand there," he said, pointing towards the sea. He then took out a small knife and untied me and David, quickly stancing back to Sonia with the barrel to her head. "C'mon. We are losing daylight," he shouted. David and I walked together towards the see. At least now we had a chance to talk to each other covertly. We kept walking reluctantly.

David and I threw our jackets on the golden sand. As our feet touched the cold sea-water, David looked at me. "Listen to me carefully," he whispered, "There is a small dingy to your right, 30 yards maybe. Just remember it. He is watching us right now. Let us dive. Stay with me." I just nodded and we finally stepped in the deep waters.

"Don't split. Stay right with me." David instructed me before diving in. We did not look back. We dove right in. It was the same old feeling; me cutting through the blue water. David's feet paddled downward a few feet away from me. Going down was difficult without any equipment. However, we both were used to holding breath for long and opening eyes under the water.

It would have hardly been 6-8 metres, and my ears became numb due to intense water pressure. I kept cycling my body down. A few seconds later, we made a visual contact with a reef. David signalled to surface. We came up, took a deep breath and scanned the surroundings. The coast would have been some fifty or so metres away. At such a distance, it would have been hard for Anish to spot two tiny heads. “Inflate your lungs. We’ll check out the reef now,” said David. We dunked back our bodies into the water. Each breath bought us approximately three minutes of time to explore. I swam like a seal and began scanning the reef.

We surfaced back without any luck. It surprised me to see a devilish smile on David’s face. It was utterly strange. I looked him in the eye and asked, “Why are you smiling?” with a straight face. His smile grew wider. He dove back in again. I wondered if he had found something. But, as usual, he was strange and unpredictable.

A few minutes in and I caught his reflection accelerating towards the surface. David surfaced like a whale, with water bulging out like crazy. He caught hold of his breath. And once he revealed his right hand to me, my mind forgot almost all the pain, fear, and scarcity I was in. I was reactionless for a second. David showed me a gold coin, a shiny round gold coin with an ancient scripture on it. It was so shiny that the water’s reflection bounced back off it. “The treasure is near.” David’s smile had already said it before.

“Oh my god,” my jaw dropped. And, we hugged each other tightly under the water.

We surfaced back again. I coughed a little because of the salty water. “Listen to me carefully now,” David put his hands on my cheeks, “We are close to it, Donna. This is finally happening. Stay close to me. Let’s do it!”

My mind got new juice. My heart was pumping nuclear energy. My body became a living source of lava. Sea water was not cold anymore. I bet that is what happens when your goal finally manifests. I and David dove back again. This time I followed him.

The spot where he found the coin was barely more than 7 metres deep. There was an opening in the reef. Close to it, we found a few more coins. The opening was about 6 feet wide. David mustered the courage to check it out from the inside without an oxygen cylinder. It was a risk; though, a calculated one. I stood guard watching him as he went in. After thirty seconds or so, he came back and rocketed straight to the surface. I followed him.

"Donna…" He took the longest pause ever, before saying, "...we are floating over the Nizam's treasure…" I still remember the exact words, the tone, the enunciation, my heart rate, and the surroundings the way they were. My world, my life changed forever from thereon.

"Listen to me now." David caught my attention. I was high on the words he had just articulated. "Now we swim to the far side of the island. It would take a few hours."

"What about Sonia? The treasure?" I was perplexed.

"I have a plan. Anish is not man enough to do anything to her," he said with confidence.

We swam to the West side.

9:30 a.m.

We reached the far side of the island. It would have been a few kilometres away from Sonia and Anish. "She will be fine." David pacified me again. I believed him. The moment was too overwhelming. Feelings were complex to explain. We lay on the beach and slept due to exhaustion.

4:30 p.m.

In the evening we somehow ignited a few twigs and succeeded in making a fire. "Still doubting my stance? Eh?" David asked poking the fire with a long twig. I looked at him with a puzzled face and nodded honestly. He smirked. "Once we got away from Anish, he had no way of knowing if we found the treasure. He took Sonia as a hostage thinking that he would be able to leverage her to compel us to return. For a moment, I thought the same. But she is the only leverage he has. If we did not show up, Anish would get confused. He will try to find a way to trace us, but won't take Sonia's life. Now we know the treasure's location. I bought us some time. All we need is to escape the island with Sonia."

I was awed at David's thoughtfulness and presence of mind. "Hmmm," I affirmed his decision, "Some mathematics you played there!" We high fived.

7:45 p.m.

We fed the fire and made a temporary shelter around it. David and I forged a rescue plan. We had to leave after midnight and head back to the place of hostage.

Day 39

"Friends forever and ever..."

12:10 a.m.

"Remember, I never surfaced and you forgot your way back. He'll buy that story for a while. Keep talking to him. I will strike at the right time." David's plan included a blatant lie for a noble cause. I was in. We had crafted two torches using the wood and cloth wrapped around them. "Lead the way to the east. I'll be a few hundred yards behind you," David said. We began packing up the camp. A few minutes later, I was ready to lead Sonia's rescue.

12: 37 a.m.

I waved my torch to feed oxygen to the fire. It burnt brightly amidst the dark of the island. The sand crystals shone brightly under the fire. The torch was burning intensely enough to keep any wild animal at bay and start a massive forest fire if we wished. David and I were ready to leave at his cue. 'May god be with us,'

I prayed to the almighty whose intentions and presence I had stopped questioning since spotting the treasure.

"Donna," David turned me back holding my shoulder. He kissed me on the forehead, caressing my hair, and said, "Love you darling."

I hugged him tightly and reciprocated with, "Love you too, David." I held the torch in front of me and began the march. David was supposed to stay behind me for around 150 yards. Sonia was probably 10 miles in the eastern direction.

1:45 a.m.

It had been more than an hour since I took the first step. I felt like a lone wolf walking through the creepy jungle. Not for hunting, but to save a friend from the pack. Beyond the illuminated globe of my fire torch lay the pitch black world surrounded by thousands of miles of deep merciless waters. After every couple of metres of crunching leaves, dense vegetation, and tall trees, I used to look back for David's presence. He was, however, far off as I could not see his torch. I halted to relax for a while beneath a tree. My mind was all for Sonia at that moment. No place for fear of a wild jungle night.

2:15 a.m.

My watch was the only constant that had remained with me from the very beginning. It said 2:15 a.m. I kept moving. The cricket chirps, distant howls from the small monkeys and some unrecognized sounds bothered me a little. At one point, I felt as if I was being followed. No. It was not David. It was an eerie feeling, as if someone or something was walking close to me; watching my each step very closely. My grip on the torch became tighter. A few steps later, I thought I heard some quick footsteps a few yards left of me. The light revealed nothing. No movement. I pretended to ignore it and kept walking.

4:23 a.m.

I was just a few minutes away from the location. The sky began changing its colour. It indicated of the sun at the horizon, eager to grow. Brightening light takes away all the fear; I learnt this that day. But it was still considerably dark. I turned back for the last time to spot David. I had spotted him twice during the long walk at around 3 a.m. and 3:15 a.m. Though, I happened to spot something else. Something ran across the trail which I had just covered. It was not David. It was only a few metres away from me. It was blazing fast. My heart almost came to my mouth. I ran towards the beach, hoping to see Sonia under Anish's captivity.

4:25 a.m.

I found nobody on the beach. It was the exact same spot where we had last seen Anish pointing the barrel at Sonia's head. I recognized it by the small boat David had showed me while we were about to dive. My heart started racing, fearing the worst. I assumed Anish had run off killing Sonia.

A few minutes later, David arrived. His torch still had stamina to burn intensely for the next twenty minutes or so. Mine was almost dead. "Where are they?" he asked.

"I don't know. There is nobody," I replied. "Hey! I think somebody ran across my path.

"It was probably Anish trying to pull off some trick!" said David.

My eyes became wider. My extremities went cold. I said. "Could it be that idiot?" I was skeptical.

4:30 a.m.

Some movement caught our attention. The sun was almost on the horizon, slowly growing bigger. Both of us turned around. What I saw then can be described as the most frightening and horrific sight ever. Around twelve naked human figures with long spears stood in formation, some 10-12 yards away from us. As soon as we turned our faces towards them, they started shouting and roaring wildly, jumping up and down on the same spot. First rays of the sun also eventually stuck the beach. Visible on their long spears were three distinct human heads.

David put forward his torch as a reflex. The men took a step back. Fear could be seen on their faces. "Who… are… they?" I asked, trying my best to articulate good questions despite being scared to death.

"No idea. Are those heads…?" David tried to put forward a reasonable question. Both of us were certain of the answer. We found ourselves trapped amidst the people-hating tribe.

"The fire will last for a few minutes only. They seem to be afraid of it. I think that is why we were spared at night. Slowly move to the boat, now!" David whispered. I carefully took baby steps, without much body movement. David followed me while still pointing the torch at the naked tribals. They measured each step towards us as we pushed the boat into the sea.

"We are heading back to the sub," David declared.

5:15 a.m.

The two of us arrived at the partially sunken N45. I fainted shortly afterwards.

Day 40

"One last move..."

I woke up abruptly. The floor was strangely tilted. I was in a dazed state, looking around. A headache made me want to lie back again. The incident, only a few hours old, came back to haunt my memory. I couldn't help but weep. I wept as loud as I could. I wanted to cut open my heart. It was a strong emotion of guilt, regret, frustration, topped with a hint of happiness.

David came running to me on hearing me cry out loud. He held me tightly in his arms I was clearly suffering from shock, trauma and mental burnout. A few moments in his arms calmed me down. He wiped my tears and held me close to him. "We are safe, we are safe." David kept murmuring in my ear. "We are back to the N45," he said. "You fainted. I woke you up but then you fell in a deep sleep," he explained.

I put myself back together and transited to my baseline mental state. The pain and sorrow were slightly greater than the accomplish itself. "I could have saved her." I wept again, falling into David's arms.

"There is nothing you could have done. Nobody possibly knew about the wild tribe," said David. "Here is the thing we are going to do if we want out." I looked into his eyes for another plan. Till now, they seemed to have worked for both of us. "All the communication systems are down. The electric generator went out long ago. We need Anish's radio set. It should probably be on the island. We have the motorboat, harpoon, and other required tools. We can make it," he said.

I was convinced. "We have to bring their bodies to honor them," I said.

"I'll do that for you," David promised me. "I'll make plenty of fire. The bastards are afraid of it. Don't hesitate to shoot the harpoon through their hearts, darling." David's suppressed anger was visible now. "We will avenge their deaths, Donna," he said.

"Give me today to prep myself. You need a break as well. Please go to sleep. We 'attack' tomorrow morning," declared David.

I nodded and went back to the tilted floor to shun myself from the reality. I dozed off soon after.

Day 41

"Fortune sides with those who dare."

The morning sea of the forty-first day was unlike anything before. Nothing seemed to have changed. Though, the air was strange. It felt like the environment was charged with extreme emotions. A baffling anxiety caused my heart to beat irregularly. Never had I ever thought before that I would witness something like this, first hand. We were going to confront the hostile tribe. To this day, my nerves go cold as I recall the objective. The mission was to search and retrieve two crucial elements; Sonia and Samira's remain for an honourable cremation, and the radio set. David and I were certain that Samira became the tribe's victim. We were about to meet the whole truth of our story.

David had prepared for the extraction mission overnight. We spent hours on the tilted deck, salvaging anything of use. The N45 still protected us from the cold-hearted ocean and any more life threats. We were like the fetus inside of its womb. I stood on the deck, constantly watching the island. By that point,

I was so emotionally numb that I had stopped caring. Somehow, I feared for David's life.

6:00 a.m.

David lowered the motorized inflatable rib into the water. It was propelled by the powerful gas motor, the same one that once helped me spot Samira in the cold sea. Old memories flashed in front of my eyes as I stepped onto the boat. On the floor of the boat lay equipment, a Glock 20 handgun, and two long fire torches. I took the pistol in my palms, "They shoot bears with this in Alaska?" I asked.

"Yes," David said as he pull-started the motor.

The boat wobbled on the waves and we were all set to go. I inspected the fine metallurgy of the weapon. "10 mm. 15 rounds. Blow one of them and others won't ever touch the alien men." David's rage spoke clearly. I looked at him. He accelerated the rib.

"We're better than them. We are humans," I said.

The boat cut through the waves, jumping from one to another. We were heading back to the place that had tried to eat us a day before. The engine's sound whirled my thoughts. The broken pieces were finally making sense to me. The pirates knew about the island. They probably left us for dead. Samira might have been dragged by the Sentinel tribe in the dead of the night. She did not have any flame with her. All the nights we had survived on the island, was possibly due to the presence of flames near us. All this made sense now. I discussed my suspicions with David. He was already convinced about the same.

The boat soon cut through the shore sand. "Keep the engine spooled up, don't let the propeller get stuck in the sand. I'll be back as soon as I can. And… do not let that flame of the torch die." David instructed me before jumping off the boat. He lit up his own torch, loaded the handgun, turned back and said, "I will have to go deep into the jungle. I don't know how many of them are there. If I don't return, head back to the submarine. You'll find a way out. I trust you."

"We are leaving together, David. Dead or alive." My grit stood for me for I was not as rational at the time, but more emotional. "Hurry up! Retrieve the packages. I will keep guard over here. I have the flame, the boat, and the harpoon…"

At precisely 6:17 a.m, David headed inside the island. I could feel the sinister presence of the man-hunting tribe. 'May god be with us,' I prayed for both of us. David's heavy body imprinted on the sand. His handgun aimed down, and the left hand held the torch. In his backpack were a knife, a few plastic bags, 6 liters of gasoline, and a rope. David told me that he'd try to trace the 'bodies' where they were last seen. The last resort would be to burn the island and keep moving. The rats would then run for their lives.

I stood guard on the boat, watching closely for any movement. I set the motor on 'neutral' and kept is buzzing on 'idle'. Minutes passed by like hours. But my patience reservoir was enormously deep.

I glanced at my watch. It was 7:15 a.m. I had no estimation as to how long David should take to accomplish the mission. I just wanted to leave, go back home, hug my mom, sleep in my room and then shut down my mind for a month. I was emotionally drained. My mental burnout, though, had somehow strengthened me to the core and I would never even think of giving up.

Just when I had made up my mind to jump off the boat and saunter around, my eyes caught a movement. The movement was approximately at 50 yards in the direction in which David had gone. I thought he was coming back. Though, a few seconds later, similar movements caught my attention from multiple directions. All within 50-100 yards from my boat.

The killer Sentinel tribe unravelled itself from the tall trees and thick island bushes. They would have been around thirty-five in strength. All eyes were upon me. My fear came back to haunt me. For once I thought that they would have captured or killed David. But I decided not to jump conclusions; partly because I was thinking about saving myself at the time and partly because I had confidence in David's flame torch. The people, black, thin, tall and naked started advancing near me. My flame was apparently not visible in the daylight. I waved it. But they did not budge.

I was about to reverse the boat in the water, circle back and gain the footing again. Just then, I heard two gunshots. Scared birds flew away from a point in the jungle not more than 300 yards away. David was heading back.

My engine's reviving released smoke that stopped the tribe's advancing footsteps for a moment. David suddenly appeared running breathlessly towards me. Though, he was flameless and was holding his right shoulder tightly. The handgun hung from his seemingly lifeless right hand. Something had gone very wrong with him inside. He shouted something inaudible to me.

"Help." I recognized the word immediately.

The tribal contingent saw him vulnerable and, in an instant, pounced at him with primitive weapons. I ran to his rescue. Aiming the harpoon with flame in the other hand was a tough job. And, out of nowhere, an arrow pierced David's right leg. He fell to the ground at some 30 yards from me. I ran to him as hard as I could. As I recollect the moment today, it was the most horrific moment of my life. David was fallen and about to be overrun by the barbaric beings of Sentinel.

To this day, I thank the harpoon that went through one of the tribe member's head. But I had only one harpoon and no reload. My flame was all that I had. I tried to scare them away with it. I reached the spot. David was in a lot of pain. A tunnel vision gripped me and I was ready to die with my lover. A horrendous undeserving death awaited me. I sat beside him, hopeless and helpless, watching the sinister beings closing in on us. My senses came back at the last moment when I saw the Glock 20 handgun again.

Three shots were all it took. The rest became history. David did not remember me carrying him back to the sub. He did not wake up until the next morning.

Day 42

"The sweetest journey is always back to home."

David opened his eyes. I was seated right beside him. David's golden hair covered his face and waved in the wind. It was a beautiful sight to see someone healing. The mission took a lot from me. But I could not complain about the Universe's plan. It gave back a lot too. I would never forget the crew, the N45, the ocean, the treasure, the thrill, the death, and the sorrow this expedition bought. "Where are we?" David stuttered under the influence of painkillers.

"In the chopper!" I replied with a smile as I slipped my fingers in his dry and dirty but cool hair.

"The Indian Coast Guard's chopper arrived at my Mayday call. We have been flying for over an hour," I said to him. "Nobody knows about the expedition, David. All they know is we were kidnapped," I said.

"And why were we here?" He questioned back.

"For the treasure we hid in the N45. Anish tricked us, and then coerced us to follow his command. Then you know what happened on the island," I said. I fabricated the story well before the chopper arrived.

"It was one hell of a journey, Donna," David said. A tear rolled out of his eye, accompanying mine. I nodded, holding his hand.

"Fifty Minutes to ETA. INS Vikrant approach clear," the pilot-in-command declared over the radio. We were destined to land on an Indian Aircraft Carrier.

I looked out of the window. A few seagulls flew in formation with us. The ocean stretched till eternity. David held my hand and slipped the golden coin we had found. "The treasure waits for us to be taken. We can do all the good things we've ever wanted," he said.

I smiled and tears fell down my cheeks. "The Nizam's infamous treasure; too great for any one man," I said to him.

David smiled and dozed off. He was too tired and weak to stay awake. The Chopper blazed through the clouds over the Indian Ocean as I watched it from above.

Present Day

"To the victor goes the spoil."

One could only hear the ticking of the clock at the distance. Silence prevailed in the room decorated with the red velvet walls. Heavy, shiny artifacts curated along the four walls were gladly telling the story of their discovery. "So... what happened after that, Ms Donna?" the press reporter got keen. Donna sat in front of about twenty press reporters with David and Mr Roengten. She looked at David, smiled a little and said, "Well, after we landed aboard INS Vikrant, I and David had a little talk. David and I decided that it would be wise to inform the government as the Nizam's treasure was truly the nation's wealth," she said. "We went back to the spot with Fort Bridge's elite team to extract the gigantic load of the treasure. They were happy to help us in return of the piece of cake. The government showed a great gesture and allowed me and David to secure a significant stake in from the treasure. Since then, the government has sealed and declared North Sentinel island under the restricted area permit regime, a decision taken to ensure the safety of human lives." Donna went on.

"How much did you score, Ms Donna?" an inquisitive male reporter asked her straightaway.

"Haha, being curious, aren't you?" David joked holding the mic. Everyone giggled. "I won't reveal the confidential information," said Donna.

"But it was enough for us to afford this mansion, start a diving school, and donate to the statewide charities generously."

"What is the name of your diving school, ma'am?" asked the same reporter. Donna looked at David, holding his hand tightly. "Samira and Sonia's Diving School," she said with a streak of pride in her eyes.

There were so many questions that people were dying to get answers for. "Any more questions for the duo?" Mr Roengten, Managing Director of Fort Bridge Corp. asked with a deep voice.

"Did you find the 'rat' from within your company, the puppeteer?" Roengten was silent for a moment. Being an ex-special forces veteran allowed him to handle the answer carefully. "We are still investigating. You'll hear from us soon," he said.

So went on the press conference for an interesting discourse. Soon after, the trio came outside the mansion with all the reporters. Lunch was served in the lush green garden, and everyone began treating themselves. David and Donna were busy interacting with all them. "Ma'am, honored to meet you," a nervous looking girl shook hands with Donna.

"The pleasure is totally mine, young lady," Donna greeted her gratefully.

"Your actions were inspiring, truly," she said.

"Oh!" Donna modestly accepted the compliment.

An old man with a blue hat, a muffler, and an old-style walking stick came over to this group. "So, when is the next treasure hunt, Donna?" Accompanying the man was an old but healthy-looking woman. Donna was surprised by their approach and turned back.

"Mom! Dad!" She went into the happiest shock ever.

"I knew my daughter is all gold," her mom said to herself. And the sun burnt mildly that morning. The clouds teased the aqua blue sky. It was the perfect occasion for Donna's autobiography launch.

The weather danced in the glory of victors, the air smelled like success. To the N45 crew, especially Donna, this day was a dream come true. But deep down inside her, a heaviness crippled her sense of joy. Donna felt guilty for Sonia and Samira. She wished she could save them. Her pain and desperation were very well covered under the shrouds of celebration.

"Hey! Donna, meet Admiral Chopra," David introduced her to the Indian Navy's commander-in-chief. Both of them shook hands and exchanged smiles.

"Pleasure meeting you, Admiral," she said.

"The pleasure is all mine, young lady," Admiral Chopra cheered his wine glass with Donna's.

She smiled at the man as if forced. Her cell phone rang, giving her a window to escape socializing. "Excuse me, gentlemen!" Donna excused herself to attend a call. It was probably another congratulatory call. Something was bothering her soul. She couldn't figure out what. "Hello, Donna this side," she picked up the call. The voice from the other side was broken. Static noise obstructed the conversation. "Hey, can you hear me?" Donna asked. A few broken words came from the other side.

Donna decided to drop the call and wait for a better network. "Hello! Hello," she said before finally hanging up the phone.

She sighed, gazing up to the blue sky. The charm of the celebration faded away. Her mind wandered into the past. 'Samira, Sonia,' she recalled. Their faces were smiling at her as if a specter had manifested itself from the past. 'I could have saved them,' she thought. The burden of guilt was too heavy. A teardrop rolled down her right cheek as Donna held wine in one hand and cellphone in the other.

A cell phone ring ensued her mental turmoil the next moment. She picked up, "Hello, may I know who this is?" Static noise made it tedious to converse. Before she could hang up, however, a voice from the phone emerged, "Donna... Donna... Can you hear me? Donna."

"Hello! Yes, I hear you, this is Donna," she tried to address a seemingly distressed voice.

"I am... Samira. Please... please... save me...." said the troubled voice before weeping and fading into static. And the call got disconnected.

Glossary

1. Sentinelese – The Sentinelese are the most isolated tribe in the world who inhabit North Sentinel island in the Bay of Bengal in India.
2. N45 Tambor submarine – Submarine or Vessel from the Military service group is a watercraft capable of independent operation underwater.
3. Oxygen tanks – These are gas cylinder used to store and transport the high-pressure breathing gas required by deep sea divers.
4. Auxiliary tanks – These are high pressure compress gas with non-air breathing gases such as nitrox, trimix and heliox. Use of these gases is generally intended to improve overall safety by reducing the risk of decompression sickness and nitrogen narcosis and may improve ease of breathing.
5. Snorkel – A tube for a swimmer to breathe through while under water.
6. Scuba mask – Created specifically for diving, they are made of high- quality materials like tempered glass and silicon to

withstand the underwater environment. It helps to keep water out of a diver's nose and to allow the diver to clearly focus his eyes.

7. Wetsuit – It's a garment made of neoprene worn by divers to provide thermal insulation, protection from abrasion, ultraviolet exposure and stings from marine organisms
8. Ballast chamber – To control its buoyancy, the submarine has ballast chambers or tanks that can be alternately filled with water or air. When the submarine is on the surface, the ballast chambers are filled with air and the submarine's overall density is less than that of the surrounding water. As the submarine dives, the ballast chamber is flooded with water and the air in the ballast tanks is vented from the submarine until its overall density is greater than the surrounding water and the submarine begins to sink.
9. Cartographer – A person who draws maps they evaluate existing maps for accurate results.
10. SONAR – Known as Sound navigation and ranging system, a device for detecting and locating objects underwater by means of sound waves sent out to be reflected by the objects.
11. Probee – The term used for a novice to describe somebody inexperienced in any profession or activity.
12. Narrow gorge – A deep narrow valley, with steep sides formed by river or stream cutting through hard rock
13. Harpoon – A long heavy spear or sharp weapon attached to a rope, used for killing large fish or whales.
14. Echo sounder – A device for determining the depth of the seabed or detecting objects in water by measuring the time taken for sound echoes to return to the listener.

15. Mercenary – Primarily concerned with making money at the expense of ethics.
16. Underwater drone – It is remotely operated underwater vehicle used for underwater survey missions such as detecting and mapping rocks or obstructions that can be a hazard to navigation for vessels.
17. Hypothermia – It is a medical emergency that occurs when your body loses heat faster than it can produce heat, causing a dangerously low body temperature
18. Fortbridge – The part of country's armed forces that are trained to operate at Sea.
19. Hallucinations – An experience in which you see, hear, feel or smell something that does not exist.
20. Buoys – A floating object on the top of the sea, used for directing ships and warning them of possible danger.
21. Rescue flairs – It is essential for any vessels that are used at sea to signal for help.
22. Depth charges – an explosive charge designed to be dropped from a ship or aircraft and to explode under water at a preset depth, used for attacking submarines.

WAKE UP, LIFE IS CALLING

Preeti Shenoy

Ankita has fought a mental disorder, been through hell, and survived two suicide attempts. Now, she is off medication, studying in a college she loves, pursuing her dream course: Creative Writing. At last leading a 'normal life', she immerses herself in every bit of it – the classes, her friends, her course and all the carefree fun of college.

Underneath the surface, however, there is trouble brewing. A book she discovers in her college library draws her in, consumes her and sends her into a terrifying darkness that twists and tears her apart. To make matters worse, a past boyfriend resurfaces, throwing her into further turmoil.

But can she escape her thoughts? Will Ankita survive the ordeal a second time around? What does life have in store for her?

Preeti Shenoy's compelling sequel to the iconic bestseller Life is *What You Make It* chronicles the resilience of the human mind and the immense power of positive thinking.

ISBN 9789387022607; Pages: 256; MRP: INR 199/-; Binding: Paperback.

A GIRL TO REMEMBER

Ajay K Pandey

Neel is a slave to his desires, putting at stake even the purest of relationships for it. When he first sets his eyes on his new landlady, a widow, all he can see is an opportunity to get rich. Then he bumps into Pihu, an immature teenager, obsessively in love with him.

A Girl to Remember is a rollercoaster of emotions, which entwines these three lives in a strange way.

Ajay K Pandey is a bestselling author, with five heart-warming stories to his credit.

ISBN: 9789387022393; Pages: 224; MRP: INR 195/-; Binding: Paperback.

OUR STORY OF LOVE

Keshav Aneel

Paarth has just turned 18, and instead of celebrating, he is driving his father's taxi to make ends meet. When he picks up Upasna from the Delhi airport, little did he know that their drive to Chandigarh will be so adventurous!

In a world where relationships are based on give and take, how their love eventually breaks stereotypes, builds a way and sets an example, is the mesmerizing – *Our Story of Love.*

Keshav Aneel has two more bestselling books to his credits, that talk of dreams and their fulfillment.

ISBN: 9789387022645; Pages: 192; MRP: INR 199/-; Binding: Paperback.

A LOVE STORY BY DESTINY

Deesha Sangani

Avanni Singh is amazed when she meets Kiran Kapoor, her lover's namesake. What is more astonishing is that his beloved shares her name. It seems like some prank by fate, but little do they know it was going to become an adventure they would never forget!

Can two couples with the same names be connected in some way?

Can love happen when you least expect it to, and create *A Love Story by Destiny?*

Deesha Sangani is a Bangalore-based author, motivational speaker, certified personal empowerment coach, and a highly influential blogger.

ISBN: 9789387022676; Pages: 192; MRP: INR 199/-; Binding: Paperback.

THE RED SPY

Abhishek Srivastava

Arya is a young RAW recruit, pumped up about his first assignment as reinforcement to a veteran spymaster – Virat and his team. In a mind-boggling turn of events, Arya finds himself being interrogated by the very terrorist he is after. Arya evolves into the perfect weapon, but will he be in time to save RAW and his country's repute? Or turn out to be a pawn in the game of master spies and espionage?

Abhishek Srivastava is a technical consultant engineer at TCS, currently heading IT infrastructure services at Jamshedpur.

ISBN: 9789387022652; Pages: 232; MRP: INR 299/-; Binding: Paperback.

HAPPILY MARRIED HAPPILY DIVORCED

Swati Kumari

Varushka is a young and ambitious girl, hoping to make her career before 'settling down', but things change when she meets Mitash. They are soon married and settled in Amsterdam.

But then, what leads them to a divorce, that too a happy one?

Happily Married Happily Divorced will cajole you into leading a happier life and take you on a rollercoaster ride of love, surprises and unknown adventures.

Swati Kumari is a Bangalore-based also a holistic healer and loves counselling and helping people in solving their problems.

ISBN: 9789387022614; Pages: 184; MRP: INR 199/-; Binding: Paperback.

IN LOVE WITH SIMRAN

Kulpreet Yadav

Sanjana's best friend at college is murdered. She was in love with a business tycoon named Nik Sethi, and Sanjana is certain that he killed her. In an effort to find proof, she decides to get close to him. Good looking and rich, Nik falls in love with Sanjana instantly. In trying to find the truth, Sanjana can either become a victim or a victor.

Kulpreet Yadav retired voluntarily from the armed forces to pursue a career in writing, and is now also a motivational speaker.

ISBN: 9789387022539; Pages: 224; MRP: INR 195/-; Binding: Paperback.